Original story and screenplay
by Richard Morris

Novelization by Hila Colman

THOROUGHLY MODERN MILLIE
*A Bantam Book / published April 1967*



*Published simultaneously in the United States and Canada*

---

*Bantam Books are published by Bantam Books, Inc., a subsidiary of Grosset & Dunlap, Inc. Its trade-mark, consisting of the words "Bantam Books" and the portrayal of a bantam, is registered in the United States Patent Office and in other countries. Marca Registrada. Bantam Books, Inc., 271 Madison Avenue, New York, N.Y. 10016.*

---

PRINTED IN THE UNITED STATES OF AMERICA

*Thoroughly Modern Millie*

# *Chapter One*

New York, N. Y.! Millie Dillmount walked down Fifth Avenue, her step brisk, her big brown eyes wide with wonder and delight, her head in the clouds. It was really true: she was here, on a glorious, sun-filled spring morning strolling down the most glamorous street in the most glamorous city in the world.

"Hey, miss, watch where y'goin'!" The checkered taxi swerved around the corner and the swarthy driver shook his fist at her. Millie looked up and gave him her bright, winning, nineteen-year-old smile. Immediately he jammed on his brakes and stopped the traffic to let her pass. With a murmured "Thank you," which no one but herself could hear, Millie daintily picked up her long, flowing skirt an inch or two and glided across the Avenue, rather enjoying the loud hooting of horns and the glances thrown her way from the gaping passengers atop the open double-decker Fifth Avenue bus.

This was exactly the way she had imagined it would be. New York would open its stylish, generous arms and take her in. Back in Salina, Kansas, three years earlier, Millie had gone to see the newsreel of the great Fifth Avenue Armistice Day Parade (November 11, 1918, a day to remember even in Salina) eight times. Her eyes hadn't been intent on the tons of confetti, or even on the handsome marching soldiers; they had feasted on the tall buildings, strained to see the clothes the girls were wearing, memorized indelibly exactly where to look for the lions in front of the public library and the strange, bizarre shape of the Flatiron building.

In that year, though, no movie could give her the colors, the sounds or the smells. She reveled in them now: the dark-eyed Italian newsboy shouting on the corner, "Extra, extra, come and get your extra," the hum of the traffic, the sudden screaming of a fire engine, a doorman's sharp whistle for a taxi; the musty smell that blew in from the rivers, the pungent odor of the hot dogs and sauerkraut from the corner Nedick's as she turned west onto Thirty-Fourth Street; and the color everywhere—the beaded dresses in the shops, the flowered straw hats the women were wearing, the bright neon signs. Main Street back home was nothing like this. This was New York City; every step she took brought with it a new sensation of sight and smell and sounds; a city of mystery and wondrous excitement.

And somewhere in this city there was a man waiting to meet her. At this moment he didn't know she existed, but Millie knew—as sure as she knew that she was alive—that he was here and that she would recognize him the minute she laid eyes on him. He would be tall, dark and handsome; his eyes would crinkle up when he smiled; he would be gentle, tender and passionate; and he would be very rich. "I think," Millie said to herself, "he will be my boss." The fact that she had as yet to look for a job didn't bother her at all. A new era was dawning. Handsome young men were staying home and getting rich instead of going off to fight the War, and Millie knew that women were coming into their own, and that a beautiful young girl could achieve anything she solemnly set her mind to.

The marquee said "Hotel Commodore," and Millie stopped to watch a group of gay young men and women go in for lunch. The men wore straw hats; the girls were in short dresses, beads hung over their flat chests, and cloches were pulled down over their bobbed hair. She fingered her own thick locks piled on top of her head and looked down with disdain at her long, demure skirt.

Millie took a deep breath. First things first. Bravely she walked into the beauty salon next door, her wide hat in her hand. "I want my hair cut, please."

The barber beamed. "Of course, madam." He flourished his long pair of scissors in the manner of a swordsman handling his blade. Millie closed her eyes, but she couldn't resist peeping, and a long sigh escaped her lips as she watched cascades of luxuriant hair fall to the floor around her. Her head felt cold and bare, but a picture of Clara Bow facing her on the wall gave her some comfort, and when the barber twirled little curls flat against her cheeks, she felt that she had almost completed her journey from Salina.

There was one more thing to do. The dress shop was next. In the sheltered dressing room of The Modern Mode Shoppe, Millie stripped off her shirtwaist and skirt and put on a short, brown silk dress that hung straight from the shoulders to her knees, banded with rows of fringe around its low-waisted, abbreviated skirt. "It's the latest thing," the saleslady said admiringly.

"I stick out too much." Millie viewed herself with alarm. She tried to pull in her chest and achieve the modish flapper's slouch, but she only continued to look buxom and healthy.

"You need a different foundation, miss," the knowing saleswoman advised. "Come here, we'll fix you up."

"Fix me down is more like it," Millie murmured as she was fastened into a flattening undergarment. "I hope I can breathe."

"You'll get used to it," the woman said, snapping her up. "Now a little powder and lipstick and you'll be all set."

Dutifully Millie acquired the recommended pale powder with which she promptly attempted to deaden her Kansas glow, applied the cherry red lipstick sold to her, indulged in a small vial of French perfume, and sailed out of the store. She stopped to pick up a package of cigarettes, and the transformation was complete. She was now a woman of the world, of the new, modern world, ready to meet her destiny.

For the time being her destiny took her from the bustling hubbub of Herald Square down to the long, brownstone-lined, somber streets of Chelsea, where she was living—just temporarily she repeatedly assured herself—in the Priscilla Hotel for Single Young Ladies. It wasn't the Waldorf-Astoria, but Millie didn't mind its rather rundown shoddiness, its flaking exterior and rusted iron grillwork. She hardly noticed any of it.

All the weeks she'd spent at Belle Weatherrill's Girls' School of Business she had typed to only one rhythm, the tempo of the future when she would meet the eligible young bachelor she knew was waiting for her, become his stenographer and thereby catch him as a husband. The Priscilla Hotel was simply a necessary interim.

"Be sure to pick out a respectable, safe place," her mother had tearfully warned her when they had parted in Salina. "New York is a dangerous place. Don't talk to any strangers. They say they stick girls with poison needles and take them away into white slavery. Keep your eyes open, but stay away from everyone."

Millie had dutifully nodded her head in agreement, listening to her mother's words but not hearing them. But the Priscilla, she had felt, was stolid and ugly enough to satisfy her mother's fears, and nothing would keep her from her appointment with the glamorous fate that awaited her.

Millie walked along, humming to herself, patting the package of cigarettes in her pocketbook, glancing sideways at her reflection in a shop window whenever she had a chance, to see how she was getting along with her slouch. After being told at home all her life to sit up straight it wasn't easy to reverse the order, but judging from the glances of the young men passing her on the street, she felt that, slouch or not, she had achieved a certain success.

As she approached the worn entrance to the Priscilla Hotel for Single Young Ladies a taxicab drew up to the curb and let out a dazzling young woman together with a stunning set of matched luggage of assorted sizes. The newcomer, obviously headed for the Priscilla Hotel, was not at all the run-of-the-mill girl Millie had observed slinking in and out of its dark, dingy, potted-palm lobby. This girl had money written all over her, in the fine cut of her clothes, her expensive bags, in the self-confident tilt of her golden curls, down to the long, slim line of her elegant alligator pumps. Millie frankly stopped to stare.

"The fare's thirty-five cents." The taxi driver, a tough-looking little man with a huge, rather ferocious mustache, held out his hand after unloading the luggage.

"Yes, of course. I'll give you a check." The golden young woman gave him a charming dimpled smile and took a brilliant green leather checkbook and a tiny silver pen from her large alligator bag.

"You'll give me what?" The taxi driver stared at her in disbelief. "Just thirty-five cents, miss. Some nickels and dimes will do."

"I'll give you a check." Unperturbed, she held her checkbook against the side of the cab to write.

"Come on, lady. Even Rockefeller hands out his dimes in cash. Who writes a check for thirty-five cents?"

"I do," the girl said with another winning smile.

"I ain't taking any check." The taxi driver's mustache was bristling. "I ain't got all day, lady. Come on . . ."

Millie stepped up between them. "Can I be of any help?"

"You got thirty-five cents . . . cash . . . American?"

Millie dug into her purse and produced three dimes

and a nickel. "Here you are." She waved the driver away, ignoring his hand outstretched for a tip.

"My bags!" The young woman called out imperiously, but the taxi was on its way, its tail pipe blowing carbon monoxide in their faces.

"Don't worry. We can manage," Millie said with her usual bounce, rather pleased that the Priscilla attracted a newcomer with such style; the young blonde would lift the tone of the place, and her very presence made Millie feel a notch closer to the sophistication she yearned for.

The blonde picked up her hatbox, leaving her four other bags for Millie to cope with, which she cheerfully did. Once inside the lobby, the girls introduced themselves.

"I'm Miss Dorothy Brown from California."

"I'm Millie Dillmount from Salina, Kansas."

Miss Dorothy Brown surveyed the shabby lobby's mohair and oak furniture with obvious glee. "How wonderful, how perfectly marvelous," she murmured. "This is a working girl's hotel, isn't it?"

"Yes, of course." She led Miss Dorothy over to the desk to meet Mrs. Meers, the housemother. When Millie had written home to her mother, she had described Mrs. Meers as being "just like a mother" to the girls, and without saying so had given the impression of a complacent, gray-haired lady with a gentle face and an ample bosom. This was not quite the truth. Mrs. Meers was considerably more exotic than motherly, with narrow eyes and a bright if slightly sinister smile. Her heavy black hair was held up with great ivory pins, jade dangling from her ears, and a huge onyx ring sprouted from her left hand.

Millie made the introductions. "And what can we do for you, Dorothy?" Mrs. Meers asked with a wide smile that revealed an alarming set of sharp teeth.

"*Miss* Dorothy," Dorothy answered with quiet authority. "I'm looking for a room."

"I have a lovely sunny one on the twelfth floor. Here

Millie's your mail. You do always get such a lot of letters." Mrs. Meers handed Millie several envelopes.

"Oh, goodie! Two from my mother, one from my brother in Chicago, and one from my sister in Detroit. Can't wait to hear if my mother bought her new victrola . . ." Millie started to sit down on a large wicker laundry basket resting beside Mrs. Meers' desk.

"Don't sit on that!" Mrs. Meers cried out. "You might break it," she added hastily.

"It seems pretty solid." Millie gave the basket a little kick with her foot and it didn't budge. "My, but it's heavy. You must have an awful lot of laundry. Oh, dear, I think a little pussycat must be caught in there," she said with distress as a faint cry seemed to emanate from the basket. "I must rescue it."

"Oh, no, indeed–it's just my shoe squeaking," Mrs. Meers said with a gay little laugh. "I do always seem to have shoes that squeak. As I was saying, lovey," she said, turning to Dorothy, "I have a sweet room for you on the twelfth floor." As she spoke she edged around the desk and put her hand with the onyx ring firmly on top of the basket. "Right opposite dear Millie's."

"But that's Ethel Pease's room," Millie said in surprise, looking up from her letter. "She just moved in."

"Ethel's gone. Checked out. They come and go." Mrs. Meers spoke with an air of finality.

"And she didn't say good-bye to me. Such a friendly girl, with not a soul in the world." Millie shook her head in bewilderment.

"An orphan. Like me," Dorothy said.

Mrs. Meers flashed her a quick glance. "You poor darling. Sad to be all alone in the world." Her voice had more delight in it than sadness. "This is just the place for you."

The girls were on their way to the elevator, Millie balancing most of the luggage, when two small Chinese men came in to carry the laundry basket away. They carried it very carefully, atop their shoulders, as if it had something in it considerably more precious than soiled linen.

"I'm sure I heard a kitten in that basket," Millie observed. "I do hope it comes to no harm."

## Chapter Two

"This room is perfect," Dorothy exclaimed, opening the door of 12A. "A real working girl's room." She bounced with delight on the slightly soiled, flowered cretonne cover of the white iron bed and surveyed the furnishings, which consisted of a sagging black mohair chair, a small desk with a black Bible on top of it, a straight-backed chair and a tired chest of drawers. "I'm looking for experience, real life in the raw. I'm going to be an actress, and I think a girl has to live first."

"You seem to have done your share," Millie observed, glancing at the variety of foreign labels on Dorothy's luggage.

"What else can an orphan do? You are a working girl, aren't you?"

"Oh, yes. I sing nights at weddings and things, but tomorrow I start being a stenog. I'll interview some bosses." Millie was admiring her new hair bob and her dress in the mirror. This was just the beginning, she thought; her next purchase would be a beaded dress.

"I thought bosses interviewed you," Dorothy said, taking a package of cigarettes from her huge bag. "Have a smoke?"

Millie hesitated a second, and then took the cigarette. She wished she'd had a chance to practice first, but bravely she lit up. "Mm . . . mmph . . . my throat's a little scratchy today," she gasped, nearly choking on her first puff. "You see," she said, holding the cigarette out at arm's length, "I intend to work for an eligible bachelor and marry him."

"You are a modern, aren't you?" Dorothy was stretched out on the bed smoking gracefully.

"Thoroughly. Women are free today," Millie said earnestly, practicing her slouch in front of the mirror. "For the first time we are man's equal, and we can go out into the world and experience life. And that is exactly what I intend to do. I want to taste everything that life has to offer. Twenty-three skiddoo!" She was twirling around, wanting to see what happened to her fringe and her front when she danced. She was quite satisfied with the effect. "By the way, there's a friendship dance in the dining hall tonight. Want to come?"

"Sure. Will you introduce me to the gang?" Dorothy asked eagerly.

"They're full of the devil," Millie warned her.

"That's what I want to see. Real life with real people." Dorothy had kicked off her pumps, and she showed Millie how she rolled her silk stockings to keep them up. "This is a tricky age," Dorothy observed, "and a girl can't be too smart."

"You said it," Millie agreed. "I keep wondering about that cat," she mused aloud. "I hope it doesn't suffocate."

Promptly at eight o'clock Millie and Dorothy stepped into the creaky, open-grilled elevator to go down to the friendship dance. "Isn't it a bit early for a jazzy dance?" Dorothy inquired, tugging down the skirt of her elegant lace dress to cover her rolled-up stockings.

"Oh, no, not for working girls. Mrs. Meers ends the

dances at ten. This is a very respectable place—you know you have to be careful in New York. You have no mother, may she rest in peace, but if you had, she'd have warned you about white slavery. We're very lucky to have a housemother like Mrs. Meers. You've no idea how she watches over the girls, especially those who are alone in the world."

"She doesn't look very motherly," Dorothy commented.

The party was in full swing when the girls arrived. The dining tables had been pushed to one side, and the room was decorated with festoons of colored crepe paper draped from the center chandelier to the walls. A phonograph was playing a dance tune, to which three couples were dancing, while the rest of the guests tried to look as if they were having a good time: the Priscilla girls were talking brightly to each other on one side of the room, and the boys opposite them were determinedly busying themselves with the phonograph records. Mrs. Meers, very imposing in black, was guarding the punch bowl.

"What a ducky party," Dorothy observed sincerely.

"It will loosen up after a while," Millie said defensively.

"I do think it is very lovely," Dorothy insisted. They were no sooner in the door than one of the girls came up to them shaking a basket. "Ten cents apiece, girls . . . to pay for the decorations and refreshments."

"Gosh, I left my checkbook upstairs," Dorothy said apologetically.

"Never mind, I've got it." Millie dropped twenty cents into the basket. "I hope we get our money's worth," she added wistfully.

"Here comes someone," Dorothy remarked, having cooly observed the room, oblivious to the fact that she was more suitably dressed for a ball than for a Friday night social.

"A friendly face," Millie said, running her hand through her short hair, and looking at the new young man coming through the decorated doorway. "Tall and tweedy," Millie added.

"Skinny and glasses," Dorothy said, preening herself at the same time.

"But what a smile."

Both girls watched the tall young man go over and drop his dime in the basket. After glancing around the room his eyes came back to them, and he smiled. Millie smiled back.

"Good evening," he said, walking over to them.

"Can I help you?" Millie's big, brown, innocent eyes looked up at him. She twirled her fringe a bit. "I mean, are you looking for someone?"

"Not any more," he said with a wide, ingratiating grin. "May I introduce myself? I'm Jimmy Smith," he said without waiting for an answer.

Millie introduced herself and Miss Dorothy. "Do you come to these dances often?" she asked conscientiously making polite conversation.

Jimmy laughed. "No, I just happened to be passing by and I heard the music. Spring, music, girls, dance . . . so I came in. Do you dance?" he asked, turning to Millie.

"Well, yes, but nothing fancy." When Millie looked up at him she made it seem as if she had to look way up from way down where she was. "You're so tall and I'm so small," was in her eyes.

"Don't worry. Just relax and follow me. I make it up as I go along anyway. Excuse us," he said to Miss Dorothy and, taking Millie's hand, led her to the dance floor.

Millie did as Jimmy suggested and let herself relax in his arms, her body floating along with his to the music.

"I love to dance," she murmured.

"Me too." Jimmy led her in some new intricate steps.

"Is this the newest thing?" Millie asked.

"I just made it up," Jimmy admitted.

"Then it's new and we're the first ones doing it." Millie's glance at the girls on the side line was condescending: she must tell them to bob their hair and shorten their skirts, and they too would have a dancing partner and learn the newest steps. She was soon aware that they were being watched, and then another couple dancing started copying Jimmy's steps. "Gee whiz, we've started a new dance," Millie said with glowing eyes.

When the record was over they went back to join Mrs. Meers and Dorothy. "I love to watch you kids having a good time," Mrs. Meers said with her sharp smile. "It does my heart good. Especially kids like you," she said to Dorothy, "who haven't a soul in the world. You've come to the right place, where you'll be well taken care of."

"Poor Ethel. I wonder why she left so suddenly," Millie said, remembering her friend. "She'd have liked this dance."

"Maybe it was too lively here," Mrs. Meers said. "Ethel was the quiet type. She's probably very happy in some quiet little corner right now." Mrs. Meers laughed as if she were enjoying a private joke. Millie wondered what the joke could be, but her mind jumped to the table of refreshments. "That punch looks good."

"I was just about to pour some," Mrs. Meers said, turning her back to them to pour the punch. "Dorothy said she was very thirsty. I'll give her some punch."

"Let me help you." Millie flew around the table in time to see Mrs. Meers open her large onyx ring, revealing a cache of white powder inside of it. "Why, what's that?" Millie asked in wonder.

Mrs. Meers was visibly flustered. "That's my headache powder. I always have it with me."

"How clever," Millie said with delight. "How terribly clever. I didn't know you suffered from headaches, you poor dear. Here's a glass of punch for you, and you take your powder. I'll give Dorothy hers."

"Well, maybe later. My head's not so bad right now." Mrs. Meers closed her ring with a firm click. "I'll use my medicine when there aren't so many people around."

Millie patted her affectionately on the shoulder. "Don't you worry about us. If you have a headache, take your headache powder and lie down."

"I wouldn't dream of leaving you girls unchaperoned," Mrs. Meers said in a shocked voice. "I'll be all right. I like to keep my eye on you."

"You're a wonderful mother to us all," Millie cooed. Mrs. Meers beamed complacently. "My concern is for the right future for all of you," she said.

Promptly at ten o'clock Mrs. Meers blew her whistle for the dance to come to an end.

"It was a lovely evening," Jimmy said to Millie.

"Over all too soon." She waved good-bye to Dorothy, who was leaving with a young man she had been dancing with.

"How about coming for a spin with me," Jimmy suggested. "I have my boss' roadster outside."

"I'd love it," Millie agreed.

Getting into the little red roadster with the top down and the rumble seat in back, Millie thought to herself, this is really living. But she had to be on guard. It was a boss she had made up her mind to catch, not someone, no matter how nice he was, who *borrowed* a car from his boss. She was setting her net for the man who owned the car.

Jimmy drove the car up Fifth Avenue, went west on Fifty-Seventh Street, and at Seventy-Second turned onto Riverside Drive. "The lights across the river are like a broken string of beads," Millie said dreamily, gazing at the Palisades and then up at the star-studded sky.

"They shine the way you do, Millie. You're a shining girl." Jimmy relaxed at the wheel and let his arm slide around her shoulders. He pulled her over closer to him. At a red light, he leaned over unexpectedly and kissed her. "You smell good too," Jimmy whispered.

"Thank you," Millie murmured, thankful she had splurged on the toilet water. She let her head rest against his arm a moment, and then pulled herself up straight. "I think it only fair to tell you I have a plan," she announced.

"Oh, yeah? What?" Jimmy slid the car to a stop at a darkened curb where the trees shaded them from the street light.

"I'm going to marry my boss," Millie said.

"Oh, when?"

"I don't know exactly. I haven't got a job yet, but I intend to get one tomorrow, and it shouldn't take too long."

"Too long for what?" Jimmy asked, pulling her over close to him again.

"For the boss . . ." she was interrupted by Jimmy's mouth against hers. "Oh, Jimmy . . ." Millie let out a long sigh when the long, sweet kiss was ended. But again she pulled away from Jimmy. "You mustn't distract me from my plans," she said. "It's been a man's world up until now, but it isn't that way any more. Women are men's equal now. Oh, I'll kiss you. I'm a modern girl . . . I drink, I smoke, I'm up-to-the-minute . . . but my kisses don't mean a thing. Easy come, easy go, I'm going to be hard."

"Your lips are nice and soft . . . you're wonderful. I've never met a modern before." Jimmy went on kissing her—her lips, her hair, the back of her neck, and then her lips again. "How am I doing?"

"I guess you're doing all right," Millie said, trying to catch her breath. "What do you do? I mean, what do you do for work?"

"I'm in steel," Jimmy said casually. "Steel equipment for offices . . ."

"You mean like paper clips?" Millie's big brown eyes were looking up into his.

Jimmy nodded. "Yeah, sure, like paper clips."

"Oh, I've got to go home." Millie sat up primly, seeing the time on the big clock across the river. "Mrs. Meers keeps a very respectable hotel . . . she locks the front door at eleven o'clock."

"Okay, we'll get you there." Jimmy raced the little red roadster back to the Priscilla, keeping one arm around Millie at the same time.

In front of the hotel he gave her another long kiss, which she returned with enthusiasm.

"Can I see you? That is until you get engaged or married or whatever?" Jimmy asked.

"Yes, sure," Millie answered promptly.

Up in her room Millie took off her new dress and hung it away lovingly. She made a mental note to shorten all her skirts first thing in the morning. In her light woolen bathrobe, a going-away present from her mother, she sat down by the open window and rested her arms and head on the sill. The breeze coming in from the Hudson brought with it a smell of the ocean, and in the distance she could hear the tantalizing whistle of a ship. The Chelsea streets were quiet, but the hum of the city was ever present. It was a beautiful city, Millie thought, and she wondered if she could make her heart and her feelings as up-to-the-minute modern as her ideas. Jimmy's eyes were so serious when he kissed her, and they crinkled up so when he laughed . . . but love was old-fashioned. It had gone out with long skirts and high buttoned shoes. Millie sighed and stood up resolutely to brush her hair.

Short hair was considerably easier to brush than long hair, and she couldn't forget for a minute that this was a new, modern world, and that she had come to New York to have her fling and to marry her boss. Romance skiddoo!

## Chapter Three

Millie's feet hurt in their high heels. Wearily she leaned against a building and consulted the typed list of names she had been given at Belle Weatherill's Girls' School of Business. Six down and one to go; the six had been eliminated by Millie for various reasons: married . . . engaged . . . mama's boy . . . pincher. . . . The last one on the list was Mr. Trevor Graydon, assistant office manager, Sincere Trust Insurance Building, twentieth floor.

"Ma'am, it's Mr. Graydon that I want to see. Is he single?" Millie addressed herself to a scrawny woman in her mid-fifties who was eying Millie up and down from behind her desk. A small sign said that she was Miss Flannery, director of female personnel.

"Why do you ask if he's single?" Miss Flannery demanded, reaching out and touching Millie's cheek to see if the pink came off on her finger, which it did. Miss Flannery scowled. "The devil certainly stays busy," she muttered, but she pointed out the way to Trevor Graydon's office at the end of the hall.

Millie stopped before the door, knocked, and patted her hair. Instinctively she pulled in her stomach and threw out her bosom, then remembering, hastily tried to reverse the order. Before she was quite sure what was in and what was out, a hearty voice answered her knock. "Enter, and fore!"

"For what?" Millie asked as she opened the door, and then stopped short to steady herself. *He* was standing before her. Tall, slim, with a perfect profile and black hair slicked so it shone, in an elegant flannel suit, a pipe in his mouth and a golf club in his hands, he was gracefully practicing putting, sending the white ball neatly into a small tin cup imbedded in a luxurious green carpet.

"I hope I'm not interrupting something important," Millie said timidly, when she came to.

"Quite all right. Make yourself at home, Miss Dillmount. Important to stay fit. Keeps a man on his mettle." Mr. Graydon flashed her a smile that was a perfect ad for Pepsodent.

"Love to be there with you," Millie murmured.

"You like golf?" he asked, sitting down behind a huge, cluttered desk.

"I adore the game," Millie said, hoping he wouldn't delve further, because her knowledge of golf was limited to knowing the one word *mashie*, which sounded a bit indecent to her.

"You come here well recommended," Mr. Graydon said in a business-like tone of voice, scanning Millie's letter from Belle Weatherill's. "Take off your things and let's have a sample."

Millie froze for one horrifying second, and then took off her hat, pulled off her gloves and sat down at the typewriter. She closed her eyes to steady herself, but her head was reeling: she saw herself and Mr. Trevor Graydon dancing together at the Plaza, saw them riding atop a Fifth Avenue bus, saw them racing across the countryside in a little red roadster . . . "Millie, darling, the minute you walked into my office that first day, I knew it was true love" . . . and they would laugh together at the idea that once she had been his stenographer . . . it would be an amusing story to tell their children . . .

"Miss Dillmount, take a letter."

Millie picked up a new steno pad and pencil, poised for action. "I take forty words a minute," she said proudly.

Her pencil flew back and forth as Mr. Graydon dictated in a quick, staccato tone. She was nervous, but she kept up bravely, and then promptly and neatly transcribed her scribbled notes on the typewriter. While he was reading her finished pages, she gathered up the papers on his desk into a neat pile, answered the phone, dusted off the tobacco from the desk, emptied the ash tray, and finally faced him with a smile.

"You've made the team, Miss Dillmount," Mr. Graydon said. "Swell, just swell."

Millie wanted to throw her arms around his virile neck, but she restrained herself, saying, "Oh, thank you Mr. Graydon, thank you very much. I think this job is going to be just dandy."

At the end of her first day's work, promptly at five o'clock when the large office building emptied out, Millie felt as if she truly belonged to New York. Squashed in the elevator with the sharply dressed, chattering office girls, Millie pushed her way with the others, took mental notes on their clothes and memorized the latest New Yorkese catch phrases. These girls would have nothing on her, she vowed, and she would bet anyone that not one of them had picked a winner like Trevor Graydon.

She even enjoyed the subway crush, although she quickly put a fat lady between herself and an evil-eyed man who pinched her. This was New York, this was living, this was being part of the pulsating, magic mystery that was the biggest city in the world—the smell of people, of musty air, of stale peanuts, of spearmint gum.

When Millie came out of the subway at Twenty-Third Street, the city was bathed in the soft rosy glow of the sun setting behind the New Jersey marshlands. It was a nostalgic time of day, full of love and expectation: couples walking hand in hand, women scurrying home to their nests laden with groceries, lights turned on, movie marquees lit up, laughter coming from the neighborhood pubs, girls waiting for the telephone to ring, and men buying last-minute theater tickets.

Millie walked the long blocks west to the Priscilla wondering why she wasn't the happiest girl in the world. Why did her heart miss a beat each time she saw a tall, thin young man with glasses approach, only to feel it drop when he turned out to be a stranger? Why did her feet carry her forward hurriedly each time she glimpsed a shining red roadster, only to fall back disconsolately when the car disappeared? "No nonsense, girl," Millie told herself sternly—"Trevor Graydon is the man of your dreams. You didn't come to New York, N. Y. to get mixed up with a vendor of insignificant paper clips."

At the Priscilla Millie rode up in the elevator feeling letdown after her first day's work. She was aching to share her earlier exhilaration with someone, to have someone care that she got a job, to go out on the town and celebrate. And all I have to do tonight is shorten the rest of my skirts, she thought ruefully.

Walking down the dimly lit hall to her room, Millie was surprised to bump into Mrs. Meers, who was just about to turn the key into Dorothy's room. Mrs. Meers flung open the door to 12A and turned around to face Millie, equally surprised. In one hand Mrs. Meers had a cloth, and in the other, a glass bottle with what looked to Millie like Chinese writing on the label. The big laundry basket was in the hallway.

"I'm sorry I startled you," Millie said apologetically. "Is there anything wrong? You're working so late . . ."

"Woman's work is never done," Mrs. Meers said, suddenly getting down on her knees. "Something got spilled on Miss Dorothy's rug. Must clean it up." She started rubbing a corner of the carpet vigorously. "Such a pretty girl, Miss Dorothy. I want to keep her happy."

"You're so good to all of us. I can't even see any spot," Millie said, peering over Mrs. Meer's shoulder.

"I'm fussy. I like to keep everything just so, especially for these poor girls who have no home. So sad to be alone," Mrs. Meers said in her doleful voice.

"What cleaner do you use? Is it something foreign?" Millie asked, always on the alert to pick up the latest trick. She tried to read the Chinese label.

"It's . . . it's soy sauce," Mrs. Meers said and stood up, hugging the glass bottle to her bosom. "Absolutely foolproof. Gets your girl–I mean your spot–every time. I'm never without it."

"I must remember that," Millie said. "You're a wonderful woman, Mrs. Meers. I don't know what we'd do without you."

Mrs. Meers gave Millie her wide, sharp grin. "I try my best to help you girls find a happy future," she said, scurrying down the hall, pushing the laundry basket to one side. "I'll leave this basket up here. We'll probably need it later, I hope," she added with a note of glee in her voice.

A woman who really enjoys her work, Millie thought to herself, going into her own room. Millie kicked off her shoes and sat down by her favorite place at the window to think. Her thoughts were hopping from one thing to another, from the slick head of Mr. Trevor Graydon, to the new job, to how she would spend her first week's salary–a beauty parlor and beads or a new dress?–but sooner or later they came back to a tall, skinny young man with glasses.

"Millie, are you there?" Miss Dorothy was knocking on the door.

"Sure, come in." She could at least tell Dorothy about her good luck in finding the right job. But in the middle of her enthusiastic report, Millie saw that Dorothy's face was crestfallen. "What's the matter?" she asked.

"I'm happy for you, Millie, but I'm discouraged. I've been making the rounds of the producers' offices, and all they want from me is to take liberties. A pack of wolves. I want to be an actress, not a fallen woman." Miss Dorothy's pretty face was sorrowful.

"It's all those curls," Millie said. "If you cut them off, they'd know you were a modern woman and they wouldn't try any nonsense."

Dorothy shook her blonde curls. "Oh, I couldn't do that. I'd feel naked, indecent. But I don't know what to do."

"Couldn't you lead them on, just a little—that is until you landed a job—and then let them have it?" Millie asked brightly.

"If I were clever enough," Dorothy said sorrowfully. "But I might just like it, and then where would I be? I don't believe in tempting fate."

"I know what you mean," Millie said, thinking of Jimmy. "You've got to fight them off, but sometimes it's very hard."

"By the way," Dorothy said, getting up to go back to her own room, "there's a funny smell in my room. Made me a little sick until I opened the window."

"That must be the Chinese stuff Mrs. Meers was using to clean up what you spilled on your rug."

Dorothy was surprised. "I didn't spill anything. There was nothing there."

"That's peculiar. Mrs. Meers was cleaning up something. Oh, well, you know what a perfectionist she is, working all the time, always lugging that laundry basket around with her." Millie dismissed it with a shrug; she had more important things on her mind than Mrs. Meers and what she was up to.

"I don't know if I trust that Mrs. Meers," Dorothy said. "She's always looking at me as though there's something on her mind."

"There is: her favorite phrase, 'So sad to be alone in the world.' I think she's always glad to get rid of one of the orphans, though. There's a twinkle in her eye when one leaves. I do believe they make her unhappy."

"Well she's not getting rid of me for a while," Dorothy said. "I'm going to get a job as an actress one of these days."

Alone in her room again, Millie felt more forlorn than

before. Dutifully she sat down to write a letter to her mother, but the spring night air was too enticing. Mere slip of a girl that she was (as her mother always described her), how could she resist the call of the gay streets of New York on a soft, sweetly scented spring evening?

Millie was just stepping out of the lobby of the Priscilla when the red roadster pulled up to the curb. Jimmy's bare head was wind-blown. "I was just stopping by to see if you and Miss Dorothy wanted to go for a ride."

Millie hesitated for only a few seconds. "Miss Dorothy came in very tired. I don't think she'd be interested. I was about to go out to get some fresh air myself."

"Come on then, hop in. We'll take a spin up to the Claremont on the Drive."

"Hot diggity, that'll be dandy." Millie jumped in with alacrity. But once in the car, she turned to Jimmy with concern. "The Claremont's pretty high stepping—I mean even if you sell a lot of paper clips, it can't amount to very much . . ." Her voice trailed off and she blushed prettily.

"Millie, a modern girl doesn't worry about that. I thought she's out to get all she can." Jimmy gave her a sidelong glance. "You look darn pretty when you blush."

Millie ignored his last remark. "She goes Dutch too. But the truth is I'm a little low in funds right now. I only started my new job today, and I'll have to wait until the end of the week for payday." She went on to tell him about the job and all about Mr. Trevor Graydon. "He's an Arrow collar man, full of zip. Exactly what I had in mind."

"But do you think you could learn to love him?" Jimmy was cruising up Riverside Drive leisurely, with his arm around Millie.

"If you set your mind to it, you can learn anything," Millie said. She glanced up at Jimmy's crinkled eyes and wriggled, ending up a wee bit closer to him. "But what is love, after all? It's old-fashioned, it went out with laced-up corsets. A modern girl has to think of herself and the future. Woman wasn't made to be a man's drudge."

"How true, how true," Jimmy murmured, pulling Millie closer to him.

When Jimmy pulled up at the lovely Claremont Inn, Millie's eyes were wide with delight. Way uptown at 125th Street, high above the Hudson, the old white clapboard house with its well kept lawns and shade trees, in contrast to the modern apartment houses, spelled out *expensive* and *elegant*. "Couldn't we just stop in at an ice cream parlor and have a soda?" Millie's pert face was anxious.

"You're contradicting yourself," Jimmy told her with a little hug. "A modern girl is out for herself."

"But this is different," Millie said and stopped short.

Jimmy lifted up her face between his hands and looked into her dark brown eyes. "How different?" His eyes were teasing, but there was a tenderness in his face that made her catch her breath.

"We're platonic," Millie said with a clear effort to control the situation. "Today's woman has platonic relationships with men. We can be good friends, just like two men," she said firmly.

"Yes of course," Jimmy said, kissing her lightly on the tip of her nose. "Just like two men," he murmured, glancing down at her provocative curves. "Come on in, friend," he said aloud, running around the side of the roadster to help her out, which assistance Millie accepted in deference to her short, tight skirt.

Jimmy led her to a table by the window, where they could look out across the Hudson and see the lights of Palisades Amusement Park. Millie's eyes were pensive as she rested her elbows lightly on the table, the way she saw other women doing, although at home she had been taught to keep her hands in her lap when she wasn't eating.

Jimmy ordered two strawberry frappés and petits fours, and leaned across the table to look closely into Millie's face. "Tell me about yourself. I want to know all about you. All about Salina, Kansas."

Millie made a grimace. Salina, Kansas was the last thing

in the world she wanted to talk about, especially to him.

"Remember, we're good friends," Jimmy said with a grin.

It was difficult being a modern girl, Millie thought with a sigh: needing to be honest and direct and give a straight answer to a straight question. She wondered for a moment if women weren't making a mistake giving up the old-fashioned ways, which after all had been pretty successful over the years, when a girl could bat her eyelashes, wave a fan coquettishly and with a light laugh twist the strongest man around her little finger.

Reluctantly Millie faced the issue at hand, determined to stick to her resolve to be an honest, modern girl and give up all notions of indulging in flirtatious escapes and innocent if devious lies. "I was born on a farm," Millie reported, "an ordinary farm where we had cows and pigs and chickens."

"But that is fascinating," Jimmy said, leaning across the table and picking up her hand. "Tell me more."

Dutifully Millie reported on life on the farm, how she used to do barn chores in the morning, help her mother bring in pails of water, clean the chimney wicks and then walk two miles to a one-room schoolhouse. Seeing that Jimmy was genuinely interested, she warmed to her subject, telling more about her life in Salina than she thought she cared to remember. "I'm talking too much," she ended up, suddenly shy. "You don't want to hear all about this."

"But I do," Jimmy said sincerely. "I want to know every little bit about you that there is to know. Do you ever want to go back there?"

Millie shook her head without a second's hesitation. "No, not to live. Maybe to see my family sometime, but not until . . ." She stopped, and, in spite of all her resolutions, her eyelashes fluttered outrageously.

"Not until you're married and rich and come back wearing diamonds and furs," Jimmy answered for her.

Millie nodded her head silently. The modern world wasn't all bathtub gin and dancing the Charleston. It was also hard and cruel and a girl could have a heck of a time sticking to her guns being tough—especially when she was unlucky enough to be born with so many old-fashioned soft spots underneath. Paper clips would never buy many diamonds or furs.

After saying good night to Jimmy in front of the Priscilla at exactly eleven o'clock, Millie was surprised to see Mrs. Meers busy at her desk with a row of apples lined up in front of her. She had a long needle in her hand which she was using apparently to plunge some fluid into the apples.

"What on earth are you doing with that poisonous-looking needle?" Millie asked.

Mrs. Meers jumped at the sound of Millie's voice. "Poison? Who said anything about poison? This stuff—it preserves the apples. Keeps them fresh, keeps them from drying up." Mrs. Meers gave Millie her barracuda smile.

"But why bother? I mean, why preserve apples?" As always Millie was impressed by Mrs. Meers' housewifely tricks.

"You never know," Mrs. Meers said quite gaily, "when you need an apple at the right moment. It can be a matter of life or death sometimes," she added with a chuckle.

"You're teasing me," Millie said affectionately. "You're up to something . . . always working. What a woman!"

"An apple a day takes an orphan away," Mrs. Meers hummed under her breath, but as Mrs. Meers knew, Millie did not hear her as the elevator door closed with a loud click behind her.

## *Chapter Four*

A week later Millie was sitting in her office sparkling in a new dress, waiting for Mr. Graydon to come in. She had bought the dress with him specifically in mind, and in tune with his athletic bent it was strictly tailored, causing Millie to feel a bit of a girl scout in it. Her mind, however, was not totally preoccupied with Trevor Graydon. Each time the phone rang she jumped to answer it, hoping to hear Jimmy's voice at the other end, and each time it proved to be otherwise her heart drooped with disappointment.

"Hello there." Trevor Graydon came in, brisk as ever. He selected a golf club from his bag in the corner, took a few swings, and then went around opening the windows. "Not enough fresh air; stale air, stale mind," he said briskly, ignoring the fact that he was causing all the papers on his desk to blow about. Hastily Millie seized various objects such as paperweights to restore order. Watching her, for the first time Mr. Graydon noticed her new dress. "Neat dress," he commented.

Millie smiled her appreciation. In the course of the week she had managed to keep his desk in order, make a list of the telephone numbers he called most frequently, learn what nights he went to his gym, and make herself as indispensable to him as she knew how. But she didn't feel that she was truly making progress, at least not in the direction that she wanted to. Mr. Graydon accepted with no comment the fresh rose that she placed on his desk each morning, and there was not the slightest hint of anything romantic in the staccato tones with which he voiced his top-sergeant commands and dictation. Actually he was so eager to treat her as an equal, Millie rationalized to herself, that he had taken to calling her John. "Because I'm so efficient, Johnny-on-the-spot, you know," she had explained to Dorothy, further reassuring herself that he was "businesslike, not cold; manly but not gruff."

Yet in her lonely nights in her room, Millie sometimes wondered if perhaps Mr. Graydon were not carrying this new equality stuff too far—but she quickly dismissed the disloyal thought from her mind, feeling that thinking such a thing, even for a moment, was a base betrayal of her dedicated cause.

Today she decided she had better start taking bolder steps. "I love fresh air," Millie said brightly, hoping that he would not notice the goose flesh on her arms. "I wonder if I could ever learn to play golf the way you do."

"Start when you're young. Keep your eye on the ball and swing. Greatest game in the world." Trevor Graydon called her over to take some letters, his perfect profile clear and innocent as a baby's. Millie's pencil flew over the paper while her mind was searching for a way to bring the conversation around to a more intimate subject than ordering new carbon paper.

By lunch time she had made no headway and was feeling more depressed than ever. A modern girl was supposed to go out and get what she wanted, but no one had ever bothered to tell her how to go about doing it. If all the old tricks of catching a man were out, what did the Twenties offer in the way of new ones? The suffragettes would be proud of me, Millie thought ruefully, for not only keeping my own name but having it changed to John!

Her spirits rose when, walking past a small Italian restaurant, she saw Miss Dorothy's blonde curled head inside. Miss Dorothy would buck her up—and maybe, considering all her travels and that she was going to be an actress, she'd have some useful ideas. Millie was just about to rush in to join Miss Dorothy, when a second look showed her that Dorothy was not alone. A young man was sitting with her—a tall, skinny young man with glasses who was none other than Jimmy Smith.

Millie pressed her nose against the window to make sure. There was no mistaking his crinkled eyes, friendly grin, rumpled hair. Sick at heart, Millie turned away, walking as quickly as she could in the opposite direction. She argued with herself furiously all the while she listlessly ate a hot dog and drank a cup of coffee at a corner store.

"You're the one who told him you were platonic friends," one part of her said. "He's got a right to see any girl he wants to."

"But," another part of her answered back, "a man's not supposed to believe everything a girl says."

"That's old fashioned," was the counterargument. "Today's moderns are honest and forthright."

"Who needs to be so honest and forthright?" was the swift answer to that gambit. "You don't have to overdo being so darned modern!"

Nobody won the argument. It went on and on inside Millie's head, but when she came back to work she took a long, hard look at Trevor Graydon's perfect profile and resolved once more to devote her mind and efforts to the matter at hand, and to stick to the goal for which she had come to New York: to marry the boss.

That afternoon Millie cheated. She quite frankly and ruthlessly decided that a girl had to look out for herself in any way that she found best, and if it meant being somewhat less than honest and forthright, the end justified the means. Quite cleverly, she thought, she brought the conversation with Mr. Graydon back to fresh air, artfully spiraled it up to include Central Park, and with a great sigh of satisfaction ended up with a firm commitment to walk around the reservoir in the park after work. She had never been in Central Park, she had never seen the reservoir, but it seemed that she had made a great step forward to a wondrously romantic future. As she typed her letters she found herself humming the wedding march and seeing herself draped in yards of white satin and long trails of tulle veiling.

Jimmy's phone call in the afternoon hit her like a hammer blow right in the left side of her chest.

"How's the job?" his cheery voice inquired.

"Doing very well." Millie tried to make her voice haughty and cold. He was a double-crosser, fickle, unreliable and poor besides.

"How are your marriage plans coming along? Kiss him yet?"

"No," Millie blurted out before her better judgment told her that he had no right to ask such a question.

"When do you get off?"

"I'm busy tonight, if that's what you mean," Millie said with some hauteur.

"What about Saturday?"

"I work half a day," she told him.

"Good. We're going on an outing. Lunch and dinner. Ask Miss Dorothy to join us."

Dead silence for a few seconds. So that was it. He was calling her because he'd forgotten to ask Miss Dorothy at lunch time—and Miss Dorothy had no office where she could be reached. "That'll be very nice," Millie said.

"Pick you up at your hotel at a quarter to one. Say, we're still good friends, aren't we?" There was an anxious note in Jimmy's voice.

"Of course we are," Millie said. "I am going to marry my boss," she added firmly before she hung up.

In the soft dusk of the late spring afternoon, Millie

found herself walking around the reservoir in Central Park with Trevor Graydon. In truth, she wasn't walking with him as much as she was a few paces behind, somewhat in the manner of an eager but breathless cocker spaniel tied to its master with an invisible leash. Trevor's long strides were too much for Millie, even in her girl scout dress, and when after the first round he whipped out his watch and said, "John, next time round we should beat this by four minutes," she had a quick vision of him running down the aisle, and she wondered if she could ever catch up with him in time to say, "I do."

After four times around the reservoir, Millie was doubtful that she would ever live to be a bride. "Sorry to cut it short, John," Trevor said regretfully, "Know you'll be disappointed, but next time we'll do a full eight. How about a bite of supper?"

Millie's spirits soared. This was more than she had bargained for. An intimate little place, soft lights, a huge steak and a platter of french fries . . . a few evenings like this (she could even suffer the eight times around the reservoir, she thought bravely) and she'd be sending out wedding invitations. "That'll be great," she said enthusiastically.

"Good, I know just the place. Mustn't eat a heavy meal after exercise. Sits like a lump." Mr. Graydon hailed a taxi, and Millie sank back in the seat alongside him. The lights were coming on in the buildings around Central Park, turning the city into the fairyland of Millie's fondest dreams. It wasn't so hard, after all, Millie thought, to be a modern girl. If you just mixed in a little old-fashioned, female horse sense with modern ways, you could get along fine.

The taxi pulled up in front of a restaurant on Broadway that had a big sign on front that said "Dairy Appetizers." Trevor Graydon led her into a large, brightly lit room, bare of any attempt at decor, crowded with tables and filled with the noise of dishes and trays banging and the sound of many people eating. Millie sighed. It would be difficult to get cozy in a place like this.

Unlike Mr. Graydon, however, she felt the need of hearty food, and her mouth was watering for a juicy steak. Eagerly she scanned the menu past the eggplant, kasha, blintzes, sour cream and vegetable dishes, looking for the chops, roasts and steaks, but the nearest thing she could find was something called a meat cutlet. She ordered that. What she got was a concoction made up of cereal, chopped celery and carrots and matzoth meal.

"But I ordered meat," she said to Mr. Graydon, whose plate of bran and vegetables was rapidly disappearing.

He was horrified. "Sh-sh, John. This is a vegetarian place. Meat is a dirty word here."

Crestfallen, Millie forced some of the "meat" cutlet down. The city was full of surprises to a girl from Salina, Kansas, and not all of them divine.

Millie had Mr. Graydon drop her off at the corner of her hotel block, and as soon as his taxi sped away she went into the delicatessen and bought herself two large hot pastrami sandwiches. A modern girl had to look out for herself, there were no two ways about it.

When Millie came into the lobby of the Priscilla, there was Miss Dorothy standing at the desk with Mrs. Meers. "I want you to eat one of these lovely apples that I have," Mrs. Meers was saying in a benevolent tone to Miss Dorothy, handing her one of the apples that had been doctored.

Miss Dorothy was just about to take a bite when Millie stopped her. "Not now. Come upstairs, I have two enormous sandwiches." Millie felt guilty when she saw the glower on Mrs. Meers' face. "Don't be hurt, dear," she said. "I know your apples are delicious, but these sandwiches will get cold." She led Miss Dorothy off to the elevator, leaving Mrs. Meers polishing the apple furiously, a look of angry determination on her artful face.

The two girls sat munching the sandwiches in Millie's bedroom. "You must have some pretty snappy lunch dates," Millie said with a heavy heart, wanting to steer the conversation around to Jimmy, knowing at the same time that she would be torturing herself.

"Nothing so hot," Miss Dorothy said airily. "What I mean is, a meal is a meal, and a girl has to take what comes along. A working girl that is."

"Which reminds me," Millie said overcasually, "we're invited on an outing Saturday, you and I. Lunch and dinner, the sky's the limit. Jimmy Smith's taking us." She watched Miss Dorothy's pretty face carefully for a reaction, but nothing showed that indicated any deep emotion.

"That's nice. Two free meals. What every girl needs."

"You mean you have lunch with men who are nothing to you, that you don't care about?" Millie asked, pursuing the subject on her mind.

"I wouldn't go that far. I'm not a gold digger. But a girl today can have many kinds of men friends." Miss Dorothy took a big bite out of her sandwich.

"Yes, I know," Millie agreed dolefully. "Platonic friendship is all the rage today. I wonder if it's here to stay," she added mournfully.

"With free love on the side, it might work," Miss Dorothy said hopefully. "What I mean is, if you have free love on the one hand, you could have a few platonic friends on the other."

"But I do believe that marriage is still a worth-while venture, don't you?" Millie examined the ringless fingers of her left hand solemnly. What would a vegetarian wedding banquet be like, she wondered.

"Oh, yes, indeedy," Miss Dorothy agreed. "No new gadget has been yet invented to replace the good old wedding band." And she left Millie to ponder into which category Miss Dorothy fitted Jimmy Smith: was he free-lover, platonic friend, or slated to be the man to place the wedding band on Miss Dorothy's dainty finger?

Millie had a troubled night, her sleep interrupted by ominous dreams in which Miss Dorothy and Jimmy kept bringing her huge bowls of mush which they pleaded with her to finish for her own good; but each time she finished a plateful, another was there waiting for her. And every once in a while Trevor Graydon rode through her dreams on a huge stallion crying out "Tallyho!" It was a less than restful night.

The next morning, Saturday, Millie put two roses on Mr. Graydon's desk instead of the usual one. The extra rose was to assuage the guilt in her fluttering heart caused by the thought of the day's outing with Jimmy (even with Miss Dorothy along). She was also bolstered by the fact that she had clearly made a step in the right direction by having consumed a large bowl of bran for breakfast instead of her usual bacon and eggs. If it hadn't been for Jimmy's invitation (no vegetarian, he) she would have gone on to cottage cheese and sour cream for lunch.

But her heart still fluttered. In a test of strength of mind over matter, before Mr. Graydon came in, Millie selected a golf club from his bag in the corner of the room, and practiced a few swings. She missed the lamp on his desk by a fraction of an inch and swung herself into a heap on the floor, her legs up in the air. She was in that position when Mr. Graydon walked through the door.

"Good girl, John. Glad to see you doing your exercises," he said crisply and gave her a pat on the head.

"They do me a world of good," Millie said scrambling to an upright position.

In spite of all her efforts, however, and Trevor Graydon's elegant and finely chiseled profile, which Millie greatly admired, at twelve o'clock sharp she was out of the office like a deer, loping home to keep her rendezvous with Jimmy and Miss Dorothy.

## *Chapter Five*

Millie and Miss Dorothy were waiting in the lobby of the Priscilla when Jimmy arrived to pick them up. He was debonair in a tweed jacket and greeted them in his usual happy-go-lucky way. "I spoke to my boss about your paper clips," Millie said primly, considering this a safe subject to keep her heart quiet.

"It's Saturday, so forget about paper clips," Jimmy said gaily, taking each girl by the arm and leading them outside.

"Where are we going? To Coney Island?" Millie asked. It would be something to talk about in the office on Monday, because that was where the other girls usually went on a Saturday or Sunday outing when the weather was good.

"Not exactly," Jimmy and Dorothy giggled mysteriously. "You wait and see," Jimmy said.

"Look at that car!" Millie's eyes popped at the sight of a long, sleek Rolls Royce parked near the entrance of the Priscilla. "Must be someone famous visiting here. I never saw a real Rolls close up before." She touched the fender of the car gingerly with one finger. "I must write home and tell Mom about this."

"We're going in it," Jimmy said casually, opening the door to let the girls in. "It's our hostess'. She let me borrow it to pick you two up."

"Jimmy Smith!" Millie stared at him in disbelief. "I'm an honest working girl and I don't want to get mixed up in any doings of the underworld. Are you sure that someone *lent* you this car? You're always borrowing cars."

Jimmy laughed. "Come on, get in. You can trust me, Millie, can't you?"

"I'm not so sure," Millie murmured. Dorothy had already hopped into the front seat, and Jimmy was holding the door open in back for Millie. "Madam," he said, and gave her a gentle push inside.

Millie was speechless. She had never seen anything like this before in her life, not in a magazine, not in a movie, not anywhere. The back seat of the car was upholstered in a fine tapestry, like a Louis XIV sofa with the two side seats matching. There were crystal sconces on each side, a vase of fresh roses behind the driver's seat, and the fittings were made of gold.

At first Millie sat at the edge of the tapestry seat, fearful that she might get a smudge of dirt on it, but once they crossed the Fifty-Ninth Street Bridge and drove out of the city to Long Island, she sat back and relaxed, and let her imagination wander freely. For a while she was visiting royalty from some small but rich foreign country, Jimmy was her consort, and Dorothy her lady-in-waiting; she was a princess who had come to this country to see how the other half lived. But after a while she got tired of that and jumped to being one of the new-style movie stars who created a sensation wherever she went, newspapers taking her picture, crowds of admirers cheering . . .

Her thoughts were far away when the car turned through a massive stone entrance way and on to a long driveway lined with trees. The tremendous grounds looked like a park, what with the smooth lawns, tall trees and well kept flower beds. Way off in the distance Millie could see an enormous mansion surrounded by a golf course, tennis courts, swimming pools, a polo field, stables for horses, hothouses. She sat up with a jolt and picked up a little mouthpiece to speak to Jimmy in front. "Is that a house? I mean does a person live there?"

"It's pretty big, but they call it a cottage," Jimmy said into his end of the speaking device. "My father used to be Mrs. Van Hossmere's gardener. She's always been very nice to me."

"Dorothy, look at it. That's where we're going. Gee whiz!" Millie was beside herself, but since there was glass between her and the front seat, Dorothy couldn't hear her.

Overhead Millie could hear a hum, and peering out of the car she saw a beautiful small silver plane circle above them and then gently glide down to a grassy landing field not far from the mansion.

Jimmy drove up to the plane in time to see Mrs. Van Hossmere and the pilot step out. "Welcome, welcome everybody," Mrs. Van Hossmere called out gaily as Jimmy and the girls came out of the car.

"Oh, my!" Millie was frankly staring at Mrs. Van Hossmere. She was the most glamorous person she had ever been up close to in her life. Tall, slim, her blonde hair perfectly marcelled, she was wrapped up in a white fox cape open at the throat just enough to reveal a magnificent necklace of diamonds and emeralds. There were sparkling diamonds on her fingers, and a diamond barrette held her hair in place.

"My darling baron," Mrs. Van Hossmere spoke in a low, husky voice to her pilot, "you must pop my ears. Those loop the loops are doing something dreadful to my inner ear."

The baron, whom she introduced as Baron Richter, blew into her ears in a way that made her shriek with delight. "You're marvelous, simply marvelous," Mrs. Van Hossmere hugged him. "And to think you were against us in the late War." The baron, a tall man wearing a helmet and goggles, clicked his heels smartly. She then turned to Jimmy and held out her bracelet-clad arms. "My dear boy . . . the grass does need cutting. But I am so proud of you. . . ." She turned to Millie and Miss Dorothy. "Two such delightful ladies. I had no idea you had such a good eye." She then encircled the girls with her arms. "You must call me Muzzy. Both of you girls. Everyone does, we're very friendly at the cottage."

Millie smiled. She couldn't talk. Words were beyond her as she kept looking at Muzzy and the grandeur of the surroundings. While they had been talking, a chauffeur in crisp maroon livery had driven up on a motorcycle and he was now holding open the door of the Rolls for them to get in. Muzzy sat in back with Millie and Dorothy on either side of her, and Jimmy and the baron perched on the side seats. Millie thought it was extremely democratic of Muzzy to let her gardener's son ride in back in the Rolls with her.

Muzzy lifted up Millie's hand and examined the palm. "Love is very near," she said to Millie.

"Are you a fortuneteller?" Millie asked in astonishment, thinking of Trevor Graydon and her plans for the future.

"An old gypsy taught it to me once," Muzzy said. "I like to learn everything I can. You never know when knowledge comes in handy."

"You are so right," Millie said admiringly.

The car drew up in front of the mansion and the chauffeur helped each of them out. "I want everyone of you to make yourselves at home," Muzzy said gaily. "If you don't see what you want, just ring for it."

A butler met them at the door and turned the guests over to a group of trimly uniformed maids lined up inside the door. "They will show you to your rooms, mesdames," he said with a low bow. "Luncheon will be served in three-quarters of an hour, when the gong rings." Timidly Millie followed her maid through the wide corridors, up the marble stairway, wishing the maid weren't walking so fast so that she could remember all the turns they were taking, and also have time to stop to admire the paintings and tapestries hanging on the walls. When she saw Dorothy and Jimmy disappear in different directions, she felt very lonely.

They passed no one in the vast hallways except a very elderly mandarin, walking by with a small ornate telescope in his hand. He was wearing an elaborate embroidered silk Oriental robe and a satin hat, beneath which a long pigtail flowed. He gave Millie a scrutinizing look from his narrow, enigmatic eyes, but said not a word as he halted politely to let them pass. Millie was kind of glad the maid was with her; she would have been frightened coming upon the elderly mandarin alone. "He's kind of spooky," she said to the maid, wanting to hear the sound of a human voice.

"Monsieur Tea," the maid murmured but made no effort at further conversation.

After what seemed like about a mile of walking through dimly lit corridors and past many closed doors, the maid threw open the door of a huge bedroom, told Millie that there was a bathroom adjoining, showed her where to ring if she wanted anything, curtsied prettily and left. Millie felt as if she were losing her last friend in the world when the maid disappeared behind the closed door.

The room was darkened by a heavy drape. Millie kicked off her shoes to better feel the heavy pile of the carpet beneath her feet and went over to the window and drew the curtains open. Her room overlooked a fantastic garden surrounded by tall Italian cypresses which were mirrored in a magnificent pool. From a turret opposite she caught a quick glimpse of the mandarin, Mr. Tea, surveying the landscape through his telescope. Slowly he swung the telescope around, until for a brief moment it was focused directly on her. Millie shivered and pulled back behind the drape.

She then explored the room; she opened the big, empty closets, bounced on the huge four-poster bed with its satin damask cover, opened up the many drawers in the two antique highboys; she went into the bathroom and marveled at the sunken bathtub with its gold fittings, let the water run in the sink, and then decided to wash herself (so she could use the thick, hand-monogrammed towels) and renew her make-up. She was beginning to get very hungry and wished the gong would ring for lunch.

When the gong did ring she jumped with alarm, it startled her so, and she grabbed up her pocketbook and went out into the corridor. She was terrified that she would never find her way back through the labyrinth of halls and turns, but fortunately she saw a maid scurrying down the end of one hallway and, not knowing how to call her, Millie put two fingers in her mouth and whistled. The maid spun around.

"Hey, would you please show me how to get to the dining room." Millie ran up to her breathless.

"Cocktails are being served in the morning room," the maid said primly, and led Millie through some more halls and turns and down another flight of stairs. Finally Millie was led into a bright yellow and white room where Muzzy, Miss Dorothy, Jimmy and some other guests were having cocktails.

Millie rushed up to Jimmy. "Gee whiz, I thought I'd never see anyone again. I was so far away."

"Yeah, it is kind of a big cottage," Jimmy said.

"It's bigger than Salina," Millie murmured.

Muzzy had changed her costume and was now wearing a gorgeous spectator sports outfit, a simple two-piece thing banded in chinchilla and handwoven with pearls. Miss Dorothy was also in a different outfit, looking like five million dollars before taxes.

"Where'd you get the dress?" Millie asked in surprise.

"I rang for it," Miss Dorothy told her.

"Gee whiz!" Millie looked down at her own plaid dress. "Here I am at the very gates of real society in a plaid dress. Imagine. I feel unworthy."

"You look very worthy," Jimmy said.

"But look at Miss Dorothy!" Millie felt a twinge in her heart seeing the glamorous appearance Miss Dorothy made. "Trevor Graydon . . . Trevor Graydon," she repeated to herself silently.

"Miss Dorothy looks very worthy too," Jimmy said.

"You must meet my friends," Muzzy said, while the butler handed each of them a champagne cocktail. "This is Gregory Huntley, my dancing instructor"—she gestured to a graceful man with wavy blond hair—"and this is Judith Tremayne," she said, introducing a typical flapper debutante, a slinky, flat-chested girl with big eyes and a short bob. "Gregory, darling, let's try some of our new steps." Muzzy put down her glass and fell into Gregory's arms. He clutched her in a low dip, and they took some dance steps around the room.

Muzzy is so glamorous and gay, Millie thought, watching them admiringly.

"I believe in enjoying life," Muzzy called out before taking a deep back bend in Gregory's arms.

"It is better to be rich and healthy than sick and poor," Millie said thoughtfully. She was enchanted with the proceedings, although she did keep a watchful eye on Jimmy and Miss Dorothy. If Trevor Graydon were there, she thought, it might be easier to keep reminding her heart that a modern girl could not throw herself away on paper clips and that there was a place in her life for a platonic friendship.

After a sumptuous lunch, Millie had an afternoon that kept her eyes popping. She was taken through sunken Japanese gardens, special rose gardens, an aviary filled with exotic birds, long sun-baked hothouses where orchids of all colors were grown; she watched Jimmy and Miss Dorothy play tennis, they all hit some golf balls, they went swimming first in a heated pool and then in a cool one.

At five o'clock Muzzy clapped her hands for everyone's attention. "Now everyone must go to their rooms and rest. Tonight's the big party. See you later, toodle-oo," she called cheerily and glided up the marble stairway, stopping at the landing to wave back at her guests.

"I don't know where my room is," Millie wailed dolefully.

"Ring for a maid," Miss Dorothy told her, "and she'll take you."

Millie walked over to a rope on the wall and hesitated in front of it. She patted down her hair and straightened the seams of her stockings. She had never rung for a maid before and intended to do it with style. Standing up very straight, with one hand gracefully on her hip, she pulled the rope. She heard no sound and wondered if she had pulled it hard enough. What to do? Should she pull it again or wait? It was an agonizing decision. Timidly she pulled it a second time and then shied away from it. By this time everyone had disappeared and she was alone in the cavernous hall.

I may just be left here to rot, Millie thought to herself sadly. So young, so young . . .

But in a few minutes that seemed like hours to Millie, a perky maid appeared. "Take me to my room, please," Millie said in the grand manner, and, longing for a pair of roller skates to take her on her journey, she tripped along behind the maid.

Once alone in her room, she took off her dress and her shoes and sank down on the bed. A bath in the sunken tub would come later, but now in two minutes she was sound asleep.

## *Chapter Six*

"Oh my!" Millie breathed softly. "Oh my!" she said again, repeating the two words over and over again. It was early evening. The first star was in the sky, but the horizon still had a faint rosy glow from the setting sun. She was at the entrance to the garden where the party was just getting under way. Her mind had run out of superlatives and now all she could say was "Oh my!"

What she saw was a veritable fairyland. The garden was in a setting of cypresses, with Japanese lanterns strung across them and around the dance floor. An orchestra was set up at one end, and a gazebo bar at the other. There was a pool with a tall fountain set with varicolored lights which played upon the water as it came tumbling from the wide mouth of a laughing golden cupid. Standing in the shadow of a dark cypress, Millie once again saw the elderly mandarin, Mr. Tea, eying her. She glanced away and when she glanced back he had disappeared.

Couples were dancing, and Jimmy and Dorothy glided over to her doing the Boston. Jimmy was still in his tweed suit, but Miss Dorothy had changed into a gossamer, silver chiffon evening gown.

"Did you ring for that?" Millie asked in wonder.

Miss Dorothy dimpled. "Yes of course, one little ring."

"You look like the cat's meow," Millie said admiringly. "Great wealth is so classy. Like in the films."

Muzzy and Gregory came waltzing by doing a good imitation of Vernon and Irene Castle. "It's almost as good as flying," Muzzy called out, "and your ears don't have to get popped. Don't be a bashful wallflower, Millie. Join the party."

"She's a pip. Real democratic, isn't she?" Millie said to Jimmy. "Only in America could a gardener's son receive such spiffy treatment from such a fashionable crowd."

Judith Tremayne, in a stunning dress beaded solid from low neck to short hem line, joined them in time to hear Millie's last remark. She made a sound that resembled a snicker and said in her drawling voice, "We all remember dear Jimmy's father. He had such a green thumb. We hoped that Jimmy would take after him, but so far there's little evidence. And good gardeners are so hard to come by."

"Perhaps he prefers paper clips," Millie said loyally.

"Perhaps." Judith's voice was a bit sarcastic. "That gross diamond ring on Muzzy . . . it took my breath away," she said to Jimmy.

"Not completely, Miss Tremayne," Miss Dorothy commented in a flat voice.

"No, not completely," Judith said with raised eyebrows, and sauntered away.

"Witch!" Miss Dorothy exclaimed.

"Oh, Miss Dorothy!" Millie was shocked.

"I do love you, Miss Dorothy," Jimmy said laughing and giving her a hug.

Millie looked from one to the other, feeling her face flush crimson, and then for lack of anything better to do to hide her confusion, she opened her compact and powdered her nose. "You're a wicked girl, Millie," she said to herself sternly, "to be jealous of your two best friends. You should revel in their young love. After all, your arrow is pointed at Trevor Graydon and you mustn't let your cupid (Millie was convinced that every unmarried girl had her own cupid of love hovering over her) change his direction."

Fortunately at that moment a dashing, bearded Frenchman stood up at the bandstand and called for attention by clapping his hands. He introduced himself as Adrian and said, "Attention, *s'ils vous plait. Merci.* I have persuaded my star pupil that she is ripe, after only six nights of study, to make her singing debut *ce soir.*" With a stiff bow, he held out his hand to Muzzy and with a flourish said, "Alons, Muzzy . . . she is miraculeuse!"

Gracefully, Muzzy stepped down to the dance floor, acknowledging with a dazzling smile her guests' cries of "Bravo! Bravo!" She's more stunning than Hope Hampton, Millie thought, enchanted by Muzzy's gown trimmed in ostrich feathers and the huge feather boa she carelessly swung around her shoulders. Adrian leaned over to Muzzy and hummed a pitch note for her, and then turned to the band to give them the down-beat. Muzzy picked up the note and burst into song, her husky voice belting out the song across the dance floor and the garden beyond. The guests cleared the floor for her as she accompanied the song with a vigorous dance, kicking her legs high in the air, giving it everything she had.

"Yeah, Muzzy," Millie cried out in her enthusiasm, and was given a withering look by Judith Tremayne. But Millie didn't care, she was so impressed by the varied talents of her energetic hostess. As well she might be. When Muzzy finished her fantastic dance and song, Mr. Tea marched solemnly across the dance floor and presented her with a handsome saxophone. She took it from him and immediately blew a fancy descending arpeggio, which she promptly echoed with her own amazing voice. What followed was a wild contest between Muzzy's voice and the tenor sax. Each time the arpeggio descended lower, Muzzy matched it with her own voice, until finally the sax hit its lowest note—ana Muzzy came through one better with a bass note that reverberated through the entire group.

"Miraculeuse, miraculeuse!" Adrian exclaimed, applauding madly at the bandstand.

"Miraculeuse," the guests cried, joining him in ecstatic applause.

"It's swell, just swell . . . it's all swell and you're swell, Muzzy," Millie said. She was standing beside Jimmy, but her eyes kept glancing over to Miss Dorothy, who was now surrounded by a group of attentive young men. I hope she's not going to break poor Jimmy's heart, Millie thought in her generous, compassionate way.

"You're a dear, sweet girl," Muzzy said to Millie, giving her a warm hug. "Let's be kissy right off," she added, giving Millie a dab on her cheek and leaving a clear lipstick print. She led both Millie and Jimmy over to the gazebo bar, and as they walked around the dance floor, Millie once again caught the mysterious Mr. Tea watching them with interest. Who was this solemn old man who roamed around the place?

"You like our place, do you?" Muzzy asked, with her arm still around Millie's waist.

"It's dazzling. I can't wait to meet Mr. Van Hossmere," Millie said.

"Oh, he's gone to his reward, dear. Years ago."

"I'm so sorry," Millie said with chagrin. "You said our place, and I . . ." She was flustered.

But Muzzy seemed unconcerned. "When I married Mr. Van H. he was a widower of many years. I came to all this as the second Mrs. Van Hossmere—practically a child —and I can tell you I felt like a crow's quill in Queen Mary's bonnet. Well, Mr. Van H., he swatted me on the butt and said, 'Hey, baby, this is our cottage. Not my cottage. Not your cottage, but *ours*. And don't ever forget it.' And I never have. Unfortunately I enjoyed his company for a brief, but very, very ecstatic period."

"Sad, very sad," Millie said.

"Yes, and Mr. Van H. hated sad stories. He wanted our place to be filled only with good fun and good friends.

And here we are," she added gaily, joining a crush of her guests at the bar. "Despite the noble experiment of Prohibition, there seems to be a sufficiency of gin." Muzzy asked the bartender for pink ladies for herself and Jimmy and Millie. "Drink up. You're all invited to spend the night. We've plenty of extra p.j.'s. Myself, I sleep in the altogether."

Baron Richter and some of the other men at the bar gave Muzzy an appreciative look. "Ja wohl," the baron murmured.

Judith Tremayne, her eyes a bit glazed from the gin, slinked over to Muzzy. "You're to be congratulated, darling," she said, her glance sweeping over Jimmy in his tweed jacket and Millie in her same plaid dress. "You do gather together the most enchanting grab bag of people. So amusing to brush shoulders with all kinds."

"How adorable of you to say so." Muzzy gave her a frigid smile.

"And darling, your ring!" Judith's wide eyes pounced on the huge stone on Muzzy's finger. "Perfectly stunning. How big is it?"

"About two quarts," Muzzy said casually, delight covering her face. "I've been waiting all evening for someone to ask," with which a stream of water squirted from her ring directly on to Judith's astonished face. Muzzy turned the ring over to show her guests a rubber ball attached to the back. It was a delicious joke for everyone but Judith, who was too outraged to do anything but sputter as she stood there with water streaking her carefully applied make-up.

"I thought it was real," Millie said in amazement.

"It is, dear. I had it drilled," Muzzy said with a flourish of her hands, flashing the ring.

Judith recovered sufficiently to examine the damage, discovered a tiny black spot on the front of her white dress. "My mascara's run onto my dress!" She cried in a rage. "And it's brand new from Paris! Look at that nasty spot." She glared at Muzzy with venom.

Before Muzzy could answer, loyal Millie stepped between them.

"I can hardly see it, but don't you worry, Miss Tremayne," Millie spoke soothingly. "I know something that cleans so you can't see a thing. Come with me." She took Judith's hand and pulled the reluctant debutante toward the house. "I know just the thing." Millie was delighted that she could come to Muzzy's aid in a moment of crisis. In the hallway, with an imperial gesture Millie rang for a maid and asked directions to the kitchen. The maid whipped a small map out of the pocket of her crisp white apron and studied it with deep concentration. "Follow me," she said after a while. "I'm new but I think I can find it."

"You stay here," Millie said to Judith. "Just wait here until I come back. Don't move." She sat Judith down on a gilt sofa decorated with golden cupids. "Aren't they adorable?" Millie said, patting the cupids affectionately. "I'll be right back." She gave Judith's frozen face a cheerful smile.

With the map in her hand, the maid led Millie through a labyrinth of corridors, up and down stairs, until they finally came to an enormous kitchen which Millie felt must be in the bowels of the earth. "I guess it's the pantry that I want," Millie said brightly, not seeing the sign of any food in the huge expanse of counters, ranges and sinks that confronted her.

"That's fairly easy," the maid said. "I know where that is. Time for tea and cookies anyway." She led Millie through some more rooms and then to a good-sized dining room where the staff of some twenty-five men and women were seated around a large dining table laden with food. The pantry was beyond. Millie stopped at the card catalogue to look up the *S*'s and then went directly to the shelf where she found the soy sauce. "Good old Mrs. Meers," she murmured to herself. "If you give me the map, I think I can find my way back," she said to the maid and marched off triumphant with the soy sauce clutched in her hand.

About twenty minutes later, Muzzy's gay party was interrupted by a great shriek. Facing Muzzy and her guests with a horror-stricken face, Judith approached them clutching the front of her white gown, over which was rapidly spreading an alarming brown stain. "Soy sauce," she wailed. "She has covered my Paris dress with *SOY SAUCE!*"

In bewilderment, Millie followed close behind her. "Miss Tremayne . . . please . . . please. Miss Tremayne, I'm so terribly . . ."

Judith charged up to Muzzy, venom in her eyes. "You . . . you . . . inviting a stupid shop girl to a party . . . you, with your jokes!" She turned on Millie. "Idiot! Don't you know anything? No, no of course you don't. Stupid little girl! Well, I'll tell you something . . . I'll tell you what's going on around here, you boob . . ."

She was interrupted by the appearance of the ubiquitous Mr. Tea at her elbow. "Sh-sh," Mr. Tea ordered quietly. Judith shrank from the sinister old mandarin with fear.

"Tea will take care of the dress," he announced in his solemn voice.

Judith shook her head. "No, no. I'm going home. I want to get out of here."

Mr. Tea bowed from the waist. "Tea will show you out." Judith spun around and stalked out of the garden with Mr. Tea following her at his own proud pace.

"I feel terrible," Millie said to Muzzy. "Your friend . . ."

"Forget it. She's a hussy. Please don't worry about it, Millie dear." Muzzy gave Millie an affectionate pat and spun away on the dance floor.

But Judith's cruel words had stung. The magic spell was broken. After all, what was she doing here, a poor working girl among all this luxury and extravagance? And what had Judith meant when she said, "I'll tell you what's going on around here"? Millie felt lonely and letdown, the way she had as a little girl when she had discovered the ordinary people manipulating the strings behind a puppet show. The party was spoiled.

Dejectedly Millie wandered off by herself to a far end of the garden. She was alone with only the stars above her, and they were small comfort.

"Millie . . ." a voice called softly, and Jimmy emerged from the shadows. "Millie . . ."

"I thought it would clean it, honest I did." Millie barely turned around. "Mrs. Meers swears by it. I . . . I wouldn't —Holy Mackerel, a dress from Paris, France! Jimmy," she swung around to him, "let's go home."

"We can't now. There are no trains this late, and Muzzy would never give us the car, because she wants everyone to stay. We'll have to spend the night."

"Oh, dear." Millie gazed up at the stars. She felt like a swimmer out of his depth and she wanted to get back to the solid comfort of the Hotel Priscilla. Having Jimmy this close, alone together in such a romantic setting, only added to her discomfort.

"Relax," he said lightly. "You said it was just like the films. Well it is. Complete to the villainess, Judith Tremayne." He had led her on to an Oriental bridge that crossed a pretty little stream.

Millie's head was downcast, her eyes on the water. "You're laughing at me."

"I'm not," Jimmy said.

"I don't blame you." Millie let out a sigh. "I probably should have stayed in Salina, Kansas," she murmured.

"Millie, come here." Jimmy took her arm and pulled her down on a bench beside him on the other side of the bridge. "Cheer up. Like in the films there's going to be a smash-bang happy ending. I'll become the paper clip king and hire you for my stenog. Then I'd be your boss and you'd be after me to marry you. And I'd say, 'Sure, okay. Grand.' "

Millie smiled wistfully. He was so loveable it was easy to believe him—even though she'd heard him tell Dorothy only a short while ago that he loved her too. It would be oh so easy to let the stars and the garden and the moonlight take over . . . but Millie drew herself up sharply. A girl had to be practical in this world . . .

"How are you going to become the paper clip king," she demanded, "when you don't care a whit about work? You haven't once asked me about Mr. Graydon's interest in your paper clips. You can't be happy-go-lucky all the time. You've got to buckle down and make something of yourself. You're not getting any younger . . . maybe you *should* try gardening."

Jimmy laughed. "Oh no, gardeners don't have stenogs."

"Be serious," Millie admonished him. "What's to become of you?"

"Do you really care?" Jimmy's eyes were on her face.

Millie was on guard. "Of course I care," she said, folding her hands primly in her lap. "I like you."

"And I like you, by jingo!"

Jimmy bent over and kissed her, and for one long, sweet moment Millie let herself relax in his arms. With her eyes closed, all practical thoughts left her head. But when Jimmy released her, she tried once more, in a weak voice. "You have to show some get-up-and-go."

"I promise," Jimmy said dreamily, his arm around her. "I promise to bring our latest models around to show your boss first thing next week." He bent over to kiss her again, and for a few seconds Millie yielded, then she pulled away sharply. "No, no. Don't do that again."

"What's the matter?" Jimmy asked.

She couldn't tell him all the conflicting emotions racing through her, the awful war of romance and common sense raging through her being. It was a fight against awesome odds, but fight she must. She sat away from him. "I don't know. I feel . . ."

"So do I," Jimmy said quickly. "You've unlocked a room in my heart."

"Please . . . *No!*" Millie got up and ran down the garden path, half hoping Jimmy would follow her. She stopped for a second to glance back, and saw Jimmy watching her with a frown on his face. From behind a cypress she saw him shrug his shoulders and saunter back to the party, to join Dorothy. Millie walked on slowly with a heavy heart, and then she started running. If one could only run away!

She ran headlong into Muzzy and the suave butler Juarez. They made a startling sight. They were standing gravely face to face in a clearing in the garden, surrounded by old Greek pillars entwined with ivy and flowers. Juarez, looking for all the world like Rudolph Valentino, held a bolas in his hands, a length of thong with heavy leather-covered stones attached to each end. With a wild gypsy cry, Juarez suddenly started twirling one end of the bolas over his head. With a leap next to Muzzy, he whipped the bolas so that it swung around Muzzy's back, then circled his own, continuing around and around until the two were bound together.

Millie watched them spellbound.

"While I think of it, Juarez," Muzzy said nonchalantly, "supper in a half hour."

"*Sí, Señora*," Juarez said solemnly.

"*Gracias*, Juarez," Muzzy said, and nodded hello to Millie.

Juarez nodded proudly and proceeded to swing the bolas in reverse, unwrapping the two of them.

"*Muchas gracias*." Muzzy gave Juarez her dazzling smile.

"*La comida en media hora*." Juarez bowed and disappeared behind the trees.

Muzzy turned to Millie. "Sometimes I get the feeling Juarez is going to take a bite out of me. A sweetheart really, and quite the most wonderful butler. Besides he's so good at teaching me Spanish and rope tricks."

"Yes," Millie said, hardly listening, her eyes about to spill over with tears. Seeing Millie's face, Muzzy put a comforting arm around her. "Moderns don't cry," she said.

With her arm around Millie's shoulder, Muzzy led her down a garden path lined with romantic statuary. "I must apologize for my guest," Muzzy said. "Judith is a rude and very spoiled girl. You mustn't let her upset you."

Millie gave Muzzy a grateful glance. "I'm so mixed up,

so confused." It was a relief to let the words come out. "It's not only Miss Tremayne, although she did read me right. I am a shop girl, a working girl . . . and I'm a boob."

"There's nothing wrong with being a working girl. I was a working girl—in the chorus. But I wasn't a boob." Muzzy had a reminiscent smile on her face. She sank down on a stone bench and patted a place beside her for Millie.

"That's right, you married well." Millie took the seat beside Muzzy. "And that's exactly my plan. And I've got to stick to it," Millie said resolutely.

"Jimmy told me your plan, Millie, to marry your boss." Muzzy took a cigarette from the stone table beside the bench, lit it and inhaled glamorously. Millie watched her in awe, declining to smoke herself. I'd only choke, Millie thought to herself, acutely aware of her lack of sophistication next to Muzzy's smoothness. "Love has nothing to do with it," Muzzy continued.

"Yes, ma'am. I'm a modern." Millie kept watching Muzzy's gracefulness.

"You're a boob," Muzzy said calmly.

Millie was taken aback. "But you . . ." She stopped delicately, not wanting to come right out and say that Muzzy had married millions.

Muzzy walked over to a nearby swing and started swinging. "You're not going to believe me, Millie, but when I first met Mr. Van H., I didn't know he was a real multimillionaire. I really didn't. He was just one of those darling daddies hanging around the stage door. True—cross my heart."

Millie's eyes were on her intently.

"I mean he didn't look like a real multimillionaire to a girl." Muzzy was swinging lazily. "And he drank beer. Facts be known, I truly prefer beer. He was a great old guy. Affection. That's what he had. Affection." Muzzy's voice was nostalgic, and she wiped away a small tear. "We became engaged and he gave me this big ole green glass brooch, and I lent it to my girl friend one night so she could impress a new beau." Muzzy laughed at the memory. "As fate would have it, the new beau turned out to be a jeweler, and the green glass turned out to be emeralds."

Millie was wide-eyed, listening. Carefully she selected a piece of candy from the dish on the stone table and popped it into her mouth.

"Now, honey," Muzzy continued, "in this case I truly prefer emeralds. But I was heartsick. I thought Mr. Van H. had stolen it, so I begged him to take it back and go straight. He laughed . . . that dear laughed till I thought he was cuckoo. He then told me he really was a real multimillionaire, even if he didn't look like one to a girl. And we became married right away. But like I said, while I truly do prefer emeralds, we could have made it on green glass."

"I know," Millie said woefully, trying to sound bright. "While I've been in the bleachers looking at life, you've been a player on the big field. But still I just . . ."

Muzzy got off the swing and came over to her. "Honest, Millie, if it's marriage you've got in mind, love *has* everything to do with it. Follow your heart. No raspberries."

Millie was bewildered. It was all too confusing. A *modern* was supposed to go out for everything she could get. Love was an old-fashioned notion. How could a girl reconcile the two? How could one measure a boss against paper clips? And even if she did let go and followed her heart, it led to only one person. But could she count on happy-go-lucky Jimmy who kissed you one minute and said I love you to someone else the next?

Slowly Millie followed Muzzy back to the party, but she was no longer in a party mood. Jimmy was nowhere in sight and neither was Dorothy. With a heavy heart, Millie made a retreat from the garden and went back to the house to find her room. By this time she was getting the hang of the place and she managed to get to her room after only a couple of false turns. Millie sat in the dark by the window, in her favorite position, her arms on the window sill, and looked over the fairyland gaiety in the garden below, tears wetting her cheeks.

Life was a terrible dilemma. She was a long way from home, and everything she had dreamt of had *almost* come true. She had found an eligible boss, she had met high society, she was a modern girl with a fashionable bob, cigarettes and a short skirt. But one thing she had not counted on: having love strike her with its sweet but poisonous arrow.

The taste of Jimmy's kisses was still on her lips, and she could almost feel the warmth of his arms around her. Perhaps she was jumping to conclusions too hastily . . . After all, if you insist on telling a man that you intend to marry your boss and that your friendship with him is strictly platonic, and repel his kisses besides, he has every right in the world to flirt with another girl.

Millie watched the party downstairs breaking up, and an idea was forming in her mind. Someone, the maid undoubtedly, had laid out night clothes for her on the bed. She had started getting undressed, but then she put on her dress again. "If it's marriage you have in mind, love has everything to do with it . . ." Muzzy's words were singing a rhythm in her head.

The lights went out one by one and the party was over. Before she gave herself a chance to change her mind, Millie rushed from the room. She knew where Jimmy's room was; she had seen him go into it earlier in the day and made a mental note of it. . . . Down the long corridor and two turns to the left . . .

First she bumped into Juarez, who flashed his black eyes at her and bowed to let her pass. Hurrying down the silent hall, Gregory Huntley passed her by, humming to himself. Millie was astonished by so much activity so late at night, only to meet Adrian singing softly, and was positively nonplused to run into Baron Richter, who clicked his heels and hurried off. Millie stopped to stare after him. My, but everybody works late around here, she thought.

She peeked around the last corner to see who she would bump into next. There in p.j.'s, and leaning out his doorway was Jimmy beckoning. Right in front of Millie Miss

Dorothy, also in p.j.'s, scooted out of another door and made directly for Jimmy's room.

"Get in here, you little Miss Dorothy," Millie heard Jimmy say, as he slipped an arm around Miss Dorothy's waist and pulled her into his bedroom. Millie could hear Miss Dorothy's soft giggle as the door closed behind them.

Millie was blinded by tears. She had seen Jimmy and Miss Dorothy with her own eyes, so there was no mistaking anything now. What a fool she was! What an awful silly, little country girl fool . . .

Her heart was broken but she clutched at the thought of Trevor Graydon like a drowning person catching hold of straws. She'd show them, she'd show them all that she *was* a modern, and that love was a thing of the past. However alone in her big room on the huge bed, in the lacy nightgown left for her, Millie couldn't control her sobs. Life was cruel and hard, but if she steeled herself she could be as hard as anyone. But Millie was anything but hard as she cried herself to sleep that night.

## Chapter Seven

The next morning Millie came downstairs to find Jimmy and Miss Dorothy at the breakfast table. They both gave her a cheerful good morning greeting, to which Millie responded with a cool nod. She was tired from a night of crying, and tight-lipped. Every chance she had, when she thought they weren't looking, she studied their faces for some sign of their night's escapade, but Jimmy's face was as cheery as ever and Dorothy's dimples and curls showed no mar of ravishment.

How can they sit there looking so innocent, Millie thought, her heart in a turmoil as she kept her distance and sipped her coffee. To do what they must have done and appear so nonchalant was to Millie plumbing the very depths of dissoluteness.

After breakfast Jimmy announced that Muzzy was lending him her plane to run them back to the city. "I've never been up in a plane before," Millie cried, in her excitement forgetting for a moment that she intended addressing no words to Jimmy.

"There's a first for everything," Jimmy said, giving her a meaningful look.

"I guess there is," Millie retorted sharply and turned away, deliberately ignoring the puzzled expression on his face.

Out on the field with the plane, they found Muzzy running out of the forest accompanied by a burly man in a sweat shirt. "Hi, darlings," Muzzy called to them, breathless, "I've come to say good-bye to you."

"We looked for you at breakfast," Jimmy said, still giving Millie curious glances as she turned her back to him and greeted Muzzy.

"I was in the gym with Cruncher," Muzzy said, indicating the athlete who was beside her limbering up.

"Always searching," Millie murmured in quiet admiration.

Muzzy hugged Jimmy and Dorothy in turn. "You're not to be strangers now. The country club's having a poor mouth party at the end of the month. We all get to wear rags. Should really be worlds of fun." She hugged Millie next. "Promise you'll come?"

"Thank you, Muzzy dear." Millie kissed her. Then, in a louder voice to make sure Jimmy would hear, she said, "But I expect my weekends to be pretty much taken up with Mr. Trevor Graydon, my boss. Perhaps we could motor down on a Sunday, Trevor and I . . . for an inning of golf," she spoke in her most elegant voice. "He's very athletic. Also a most mature gentleman, in contrast to the flighty butterfly boys one meets nowadays . . . And the best looking thing ever."

Muzzy glanced at Jimmy in surprise. "Yes, well, of course, Millie darling . . ."

Jimmy returned Muzzy's look with a shrug.

"Okay, okay," Cruncher grunted, eager to get on with his running.

"Okay, okay," Muzzy echoed him. "Good-bye Millie, and don't forget your way back to this sea of booze and jazz."

Millie hugged Muzzy warmly. "You're so worth-while. Good-bye."

Millie turned and walked over to the plane, knowing that the eyes of Jimmy, Muzzy and Miss Dorothy were following her, undoubtedly trying to fathom her new cloak of reserve. They'll never know, Millie thought with firm determination, that beneath my proud exterior lies a poor, broken heart. She held her head high, but the tears smarting her eyes did not come from the breeze of the propeller, which Jimmy had started whirling.

Millie sat silently for the plane ride, fluctuating in her emotions between the thrill of the trip and her own misery. When they arrived at the airport and Jimmy led them to the little red roadster, it was almost more than she could bear. The night of the Claremont Inn was a poignant memory. In her frustration she turned to Jimmy impatiently. "Isn't it time you had something of your own —always borrowing other people's cars and planes!"

"Yes, ma'am," Jimmy said, trying to hold her eyes.

Regretting her outburst, Millie turned away and jumped into the rumble seat, leaving the front free for Dorothy to sit beside Jimmy. In front of the Hotel Priscilla, the roadster barely came to a stop before Millie jumped out and went striding off to the entrance. She stopped only long enough to turn to Jimmy and say in a cold voice, "Good-bye, Mr. Smith. Thank you so much . . . It was an experience."

"Millie . . . hey Millie, I'll call you," Jimmy shouted after her, but Millie went through the door not heeding him. She strode past the two little Chinese men peering from behind a potted palm in the lobby and rang for the elevator. She wondered idly for a moment why Mrs. Meers was not in her usual place at the desk.

Millie was still waiting for the elevator when Miss Dorothy came in and joined her. Millie stood silently, wishing the elevator would hurry up and get there.

"Are you feeling quite well?" Miss Dorothy asked solicitously.

"Quite, thank you." Millie maintained her cool tone.

"I thought perhaps your tummy was upset."

"No, my *tummy* isn't upset," Millie said firmly, giving Miss Dorothy a side glance, still searching avidly for a sign of ravage on Miss Dorothy's fair face. She has certainly lived this weekend, Millie thought, but it doesn't show through all those curls.

The elevator finally came, and when the girls stepped into it, Miss Dorothy pursued the conversation. "Is there something you'd like to tell me? Something bothering you?"

"No, there's nothing on *my* conscience," Millie said pointedly. Two girls got on at the second floor and rode up with them. Millie remained silent, tapping her foot nervously. When Millie and Miss Dorothy got out on their floor, Millie resumed the tense conversation. "Perhaps there's something you'd like to tell *me*, Miss Dorothy. Something bothering *you*, perhaps?"

"Well . . . I . . . I don't know. . . ." Miss Dorothy was hesitant.

"Go ahead. Spill it out."

"Well, I am terribly upset about . . . about my career."

Millie was incredulous. "Your *career!*"

"The world of the stage doesn't seem to want me," Miss Dorothy confessed.

"That's because they don't know you," Millie said accusingly. "You should cut your hair. Let them see the real you—how truly abandoned you are."

Miss Dorothy was shocked. "Cut my hair! Never!"

Millie paused in front of her door. "People can't find the real you through all those curls. Good night," she said curtly and closed the door behind her.

But she opened it a few seconds later in answer to a piercing scream from Miss Dorothy. The two girls fell into each other's arms.

"What's the matter? What happened?" Millie asked in alarm.

"My room! My room, in my room . . ." Miss Dorothy gasped. Millie pushed past her into the room to see

Mrs. Meers stretched out on the bed, snoring away, with a large bed doll closely resembling Miss Dorothy clutched in one hand, and a spray gun in the other.

"Mrs. Meers!" Millie exclaimed in astonishment.

"Yes, in *my* room, asleep on *my* bed. Really!" Miss Dorothy was beside herself.

Millie took the spray gun and put it aside. "She works a very long day I know, poor dear. I'm sure she didn't mean any harm. Just overworking. But everybody seems to be working late these days." She let out a long yawn. "Well, good night." Millie started for the door.

"But what am I going to do?" Dorothy asked in distress. At that moment Mrs. Meers rolled onto her side, pulling the bedspread up over her, obviously snuggling in for the night. Miss Dorothy ran after Millie. "Millie, please, could I spend the night with you?"

Millie looked at her uncertainly. "Well . . ."

"Please," Dorothy asked pleadingly. "It would give us a chance to talk. And if we're to save our relationship, we do need to talk. Have I done something terrible to you? Tell me, please. A girl friend is something new and precious to me. I don't want to lose you."

Miss Dorothy's words made Millie feel suddenly ashamed and confused. "No, you haven't done anything terrible to me. After all, I have my plans . . . and I'm sorry. Gee whiz, your friendship is precious to me too. Of course you can spend the night with me."

"Thank you." Miss Dorothy ran back to her room for her night clothes.

"But there'll be no more talk," Millie said when Dorothy returned and she was getting undressed. "I'm not my brother's keeper, am I? You take the bed, I'll sleep on the floor."

"It will be just the other way around," Miss Dorothy said.

"No, I insist." Millie was firm, adding, to herself, "To make up for my lack of gypsy spirit. You can take the girl out of Kansas, but you can't take the Kansas out of the girl."

Miss Dorothy ran back to her room for her toothbrush, and switched off the light. "Most irregular," she murmured. "I don't care how middle-class a place it is."

Millie was standing by her window, sleepy but thoughtful. "I really must callous up," she said to herself sternly. "Starting tomorrow I am going to be unspeakably fatal."

Before settling down on her blanket on the floor, Millie heard a noise out in the hall and opened her door to peek out. To her great surprise she saw the two little Chinese men pushing the big laundry basket out of Miss Dorothy's darkened room. From a crack in the door she watched them push the basket—squeak, squeak!—down the hall. "People certainly do work late all over," Millie said to herself and settled down in her corner for the night.

Millie woke up the next morning with a bit of an aching back, but she didn't mind. It was a pleasure to have Miss Dorothy's curls spread out on her pillow, and the two girls were very sweetie-pie to each other.

"Thank you so much," Dorothy said, kissing Millie good-bye. "You to your office and me back to my rounds."

"I wonder if Mrs. Meers is still in your room," Millie said thoughtfully.

Dorothy was indignant. "She'd better not be."

Millie went with her to look, and both girls were relieved to see only a large dent where Mrs. Meers had been.

Millie dressed and went downstairs. She was slightly surprised again not to see Mrs. Meers at her desk. Poor thing works too hard, Millie thought.

Gaily Millie went through the swinging doors and out to the street, and started walking. At that moment, with a great screeching of brakes a Chinese laundry truck pulled to a stop in front of the hotel. Millie stopped to watch the two little Chinese laundrymen (they certainly get around, she thought) hop out and run around to the back. They swung open the doors, and to Millie's speechless surprise, there sat Mrs. Meers on an upright chair in the back of the empty truck. She was obviously very angry, and swatted the proffered hands of the chagrined little men.

Millie heard a spout of Chinese coming out of Mrs. Meers' mouth as she hopped out of the back of the truck and walked indignantly into the hotel without even noticing Millie.

She has other things on her mind, Millie decided, highly impressed with Mrs. Meers knowledge of Chinese. She also is very conscientious about her wash. Imagine, going inside the laundry truck! The city was full of new and wondrous things.

## *Chapter Eight*

A few days later Millie was elated because she was beginning to see a small sign of success in the working of her plan. With one thing and another she had managed to get Trevor Graydon to practice golf strokes with her in the office. To Trevor Graydon it was golf, to Millie Dillmount it was romance.

For one thing the position assumed was very friendly: Mr. Graydon stood behind her very close, body to body, his arms around her, guiding her swing of the golf club. Millie found it enthralling. For a moment she leaned back against his virile chest, dreaming dreams.

"You've got to loosen up your swing there, John," Mr. Graydon was saying. "But you do have rhythm."

"I studied ballroom and tap back home," Millie said eagerly.

"Just swing easily with your drive. Swell, that's swell. Always keep your eye on the ball." He moved her arms vigorously in a simulated drive.

This was the moment Millie had been waiting for. "Mr. Graydon, my friend is—my new friend is . . . she's really quite delightful . . . and well, she has this golf course of her very own, and it would be perfectly acceptable to her if we—you and I—oh, dear . . ." Millie was interrupted by the ringing of her phone in the outer office.

Mr. Graydon dropped her arms and started for his desk. She had gotten this far, and Millie didn't want to lose her chance. She hesitated to leave to answer the phone.

"Your phone, John," Mr. Graydon said in a businesslike tone of voice.

"Oh, yes sir . . . but as I was saying . . . like on a Sunday? I asked her and if you'd like . . ." She broke off abruptly, seeing Mr. Graydon's displeasure at her lingering. "Yes, sir." Millie darted out of his office, carefully closing the door behind her, to answer the insistent phone.

She was wild when she heard Jimmy's voice at the other end. "Jimmy! You are always interrupting my life! Stop it! Just stop it!"

"What'd I do? What'd I do?" Jimmy's voice was pleading. "Just tell me please, what's happened?"

"*I* have work to do," Millie said coldly. "I presume you have work to do. *Do it* and leave me alone!" And she slammed the phone back on its hook.

Millie set her lips in a firm line. A plan was a plan was a plan. With a bang she opened her desk drawer and whipped out her lipstick, rouge and a tiny bottle of "French" perfume labelled "'*Je t'aime*." She applied all three liberally, daubing her knees and elbows with the perfume. She then marched back to Trevor Graydon's office and tapped gently on the door.

"Front and enter," he responded, engrossed in his work at his desk.

"Do you have a mo . . . ?" Millie asked in a purring voice.

"A what?"

"A moment. I would just love to get a man's opinion of Rudolph Valentino."

Trevor Graydon frowned at such frivolity and made a low, grunting sound.

"I mean, in *The Shiek*, he takes Agnes Ayres by brute force and she enjoys it." Millie batted her eye lashes. "She enjoys it a *lot*. What is your opinion of brute force, Mr. Graydon?"

Mr. Graydon pondered the subject gravely for several moments. Finally he gave Millie his considered opinion on the matter. "Well, I'm not for it. Not at all. That is not what women really want today. Give them a virtuous, clean, honest hero. The late War has upset them. They believed all those glorious slogans—believed that their men were fighting for only the highest moral reasons. Now they are disillusioned. They yearn for truth. Give them a young man they can trust . . . Tom Sawyer at twenty."

"I never read *Tom Sawyer*. Was he sexy?" Millie asked in a seductive voice.

"He was only *twelve!*" Trevor Graydon exclaimed in a shocked voice.

"So? If you got it, you got it," Millie said in a flip voice with a grin.

"Why, John!" Mr. Graydon's handsome face was stern.

"Yes, sir." Millie retreated out of the door. He was not an easy man to get to, she was thinking, going over to her own desk with a preoccupied little frown. She fairly bumped into Jimmy, who was leaning against her desk.

"Take you to lunch?" he asked nonchalantly.

"Mr. Smith, you are not going to *take* me again. Ever. Any place." Millie's eyes were flashing.

"Millie, at least explain yourself, please!" He was no longer casual.

"I don't think I have to explain anything," Millie said coolly. "Each to his own," she added enigmatically.

"I don't know what you're talking about. Come and tell me all about it at lunch." Jimmy's boyish face was mystified.

At that moment Trevor Graydon's head shot out the door. "John, ring my club and reserve a handball court for six-fifteen. That's a swell scout. Got to work up a good sweat . . . edgy in the gut you know."

"I have work to do," Millie told Jimmy, deliberately turning her back to him and reaching for the telephone.

With a heavy heart she heard him retreat to the door and slam it behind him. Life was cruel, life was earnest. It was a tough world and a modern girl had to be hard as nails to get along. Millie opened her desk drawer and stared at the label on her perfume: "*Je t'aime*." *Je t'aime*. Was she using the right perfume for the wrong man?

At six o'clock that afternoon Millie came out of the office building to keep an appointment with Miss Dorothy. She had finally persuaded Miss Dorothy that her old-fashioned curls would get her nowhere, and to make her mark as an actress there was nothing to do but to bob her hair. If the thought had fleetingly occurred to Millie that a shorn Miss Dorothy might have a different effect on Jimmy, she had hastily thrust such a disloyal notion aside.

Millie scanned the crowded sidewalk for a glimpse of Miss Dorothy and was not unduly surprised to see her drive up in a cab. Behind the taxi was the familiar Chinese laundry truck, with the two little Chinese men in front. Millie waved to them in recognition as she went up to Dorothy in the cab, and was somewhat startled to see the Chinese men duck beneath the windshield. Such strange little men, she thought. The mysterious East. Probably very shy, poor things.

"You want a pen?" The taxi driver was asking Miss Dorothy. It was the same driver she had had before.

"How much?" Millie asked in a resigned voice.

"Twenty-five."

Millie fished in her purse for some change and was rewarded with a gorgeous smile from Miss Dorothy and a murmured, "Thank you Millie, dear."

Millie finally dug up two nickels, a dime and five pennies and carefully counted them out into the weary driver's hand. She then turned to Dorothy who was stepping out of the cab with an incredulous and strangely fixed expression on her face. Millie turned around to see what could bring such a rarefied aura to Miss Dorothy's complacent face and was astonished to see Trevor Graydon standing behind her, hat in hand, staring as if in a trance at Miss Dorothy.

"Did I forget something?" Millie asked in a startled voice.

"No, no . . . oh, yes, you did. You forgot to introduce me to your exquisite friend." Mr. Graydon was still gaping.

"Oh, this is Miss Dorothy Brown, from the Priscilla Hotel. Miss Dorothy, this is my boss, Mr. Trevor Graydon."

Miss Dorothy acknowledged the introduction by lowering her eyes and blushing beautifully, making a charming effect by no means lost to Mr. Graydon.

"We're just on our way over to the Madcap Beauty Spot," Millie explained hastily. "Miss Dorothy is going to have her hair smartly bobbed."

Mr. Graydon was horrified. "Bobbed! With your beauty!"

"Mr. Graydon, behave," Miss Dorothy admonished.

"You could make even the moon and the stars behave," Mr. Graydon said grandly, delighted to see Miss Dorothy blush again.

"Miss Dorothy is an actress," Millie stated. "And the way the theater is today, so rotten . . . well, we talked it over and she feels she might have a . . ." Millie stopped short, aware that no one was listening to her, as Miss Dorothy and Trevor Graydon's eyes were locked in a mutual trance that had transported them to a never never land. She knocks them all dead, Millie thought ruefully, running her hand through her own bobbed hair. Maybe it is those curls.

"You wouldn't rob some lucky stiff of playing with all those adorable curls," Mr. Graydon finally said, and Millie jumped for fear he was reading her mind.

"Well, I thought if she . . ." Millie stammered.

"Chuck it, John. Just chuck it."

"Mr. Graydon calls me John, you see, because . . ." Millie found she was still talking to herself.

"John," Trevor Graydon's eyes did not leave Miss Dorothy's face, "you and I are going to take Miss Dorothy to dinner and try our best to talk her out of doing mankind such a disservice. May I take the liberty of asking you to dine, Miss Dorothy?" He might have been gazing at a goddess.

"You may," Miss Dorothy said softly.

"And what about your sweat, Mr. Graydon?" Millie asked efficiently.

"Cancel it." He addressed himself to Miss Dorothy: "Swell. We'll have dinner and after a bit of vaudeville at the Hippodrome. If the comics aren't on . . . the humor can be a bit too ribald for a lady's ear."

"What with your gut so edgy, I hate for you to interrupt your plans," Millie said insistently.

Mr. Graydon gave her a withering look. Undaunted, Millie changed her approach. "But a dinner and a show certainly would be a treat, wouldn't it Miss Dorothy?"

"Perfect." Miss Dorothy was smiling at Trevor Graydon. "But I would feel more comfortable in a suitable frock."

" 'Twill be gilding the lily, Miss Dorothy; but of course we'll stop at your hotel." He bowed from the waist and stepped over to the curb to hail a cab.

"My first date with Trevor Graydon," Millie said to Miss Dorothy with her customary eagerness of wanting to join the party. Back in Kansas they used to say if you can't lick 'em, join 'em. A pretty wise idea, Millie decided, sitting herself in the cab between Miss Dorothy and Mr. Graydon.

Millie was again sitting in the middle that evening in a box at the Hippodrome, enthralled watching the dog act. She sat at the edge of her seat, leaning over the rail, for the moment oblivious to the surreptitious glances and sighs of love passing behind her back between Miss Dorothy and Trevor Graydon. Mr. Graydon could barely pull his eyes away from the delectable Miss Dorothy, done up for the occasion like a candy box on Valentine's Day.

"Gee whiz! Aren't they the cat's meow?" Millie said gleefully, eliciting no response from her companions, who were in a world of their own. "I guess I should say the dog's meow," Millie added with a giggle. Millie applauded the act vigorously when it came to an end.

Immediately after the dog act exited, the act cards at either side of the stage changed to read "THE BERNINI BROTHERS, HUMAN YO-YO'S." Five big Bernini brothers came bouncing onto the stage, tumbling and twirling, clapping their hands and shouting, and fairly bursting out of their skintight white costumes. The music accompanying them built up to a deafening crescendo of drums, and then for a split second there was silence before a cannon, rolled on to one side of the stage, fired. It boomed forth with a tremendous bang as a body was catapulted from its mouth. The body sailed gracefully across the stage, shrieking in ecstasy, to be caught in the arms of the biggest Bernini brother. The human cannon ball, a lovely lady with golden curls and clad in glittering pink tights, bowed and waved to the audience.

"My goodness, it's Muzzy!" Miss Dorothy exclaimed.

"My, what a full life she leads." Millie watched, fascinated, as the Bernini brothers flung Muzzy from one man to another and finally ended up a human pyramid with Muzzy looking fabulous posing at the top and clapping her hands and shouting "*Ecco! Ecco!*"

In a few seconds she made a dive from the pinnacle into the arms of three of the brothers, who then performed their famous yo-yo maneuver. They finally left the stage bowing to a loud burst of music. The audience was going wild with applause.

"We must go backstage to see Muzzy," Millie said

eagerly. "Imagine Muzzy doing all that. She is terrific."

"Yes, of course," Miss Dorothy said absently, giving Trevor Graydon demure glances.

Escorted by an usher, Millie led the other two backstage to Muzzy's dressing room. She introduced Trevor Graydon with a proprietary air. "My boss and my good friend," she said meaningfully to Muzzy. Muzzy gave Trevor Graydon her dazzling smile, and gave Millie a quick nod of approval.

"Muzzy, we loved you and the human yo-yo's. You were fabulous," Millie hugged her.

"They're so very sweet. Before I met them I was quite sure Baron Richter's loop the loops had done permanent damage to my inner ear. The Bernini brothers have worked miracles."

"You were swell, just swell," Trevor Graydon said.

"Perfect," agreed Miss Dorothy.

"I'm learning," Muzzy said modestly.

"Hadn't we best be leaving?" Miss Dorothy exchanged glances with Trevor Graydon. "I'm sure Muzzy has her practicing to do."

"I'm through for tonight. You can take just so much yo-yo."

"Well we must be on our way." She was smiling up at Trevor Graydon. "Tomorrow is a working day. Good night, Muzzy."

Miss Dorothy left the dressing room, with Mr. Graydon quick to follow behind her. Muzzy watched them with a keen eye, while Millie tried not wholly successfully to look nonchalant. Millie was about to leave too when Muzzy called her. "Millie dear, would you mind assisting me for a second with these nasty little hooks?" Muzzy offered Millie her back.

"Oh, surely." Millie called out the door, "Be right with you kids." She bent to unhook the back of Muzzy's tights.

"He is divine," Muzzy commented, her eyes thoughtful.

"Thank you. I'm falling in love with him like you said was so important," Millie stated, glad that she was behind Muzzy so that Muzzy could not see her face.

"I had no idea Miss Dorothy and Mr. Graydon were such good friends," Muzzy remarked.

"They're not. They just met." Millie fussed with the last hook. She was *not* going to cry on Muzzy's shoulder again. Was she going to spend the rest of her life losing men to Miss Dorothy's curls, she wondered gloomily. Perhaps if she had not bobbed her own hair . . . well, it was too late for that. No use crying over spilled hair. Being modern was also being brave, and no use blubbering out all over someone just because she was fabulous and sympathetic.

"There, you're unhooked," Millie said in an odd voice.

"Thank you Millie." Muzzy didn't say anything, but her eyes were still thoughtful.

Millie found Miss Dorothy and Trevor Graydon outside waiting for her, deeply engrossed in a conversation which abruptly ceased when she joined them. But the rapt expression on their faces did not escape Millie's eyes. This time she got into the taxi first and sat in the far corner, with Trevor Graydon between her and Miss Dorothy.

"It was a lovely evening," Millie said when Mr. Graydon deposited them at the entrance of the Priscilla. "Thank you."

Miss Dorothy was more effusive in her thanks for the evening, and Trevor Graydon held Miss Dorothy's hand so long Millie wondered if the three of them were going to stand there all night.

Millie was silent going up in the elevator. What was there to say to a rapturous face surrounded by golden curls?

"It was a glorious evening, Millie. You are very lucky to have found a boss like Mr. Graydon. He is a perfect gentleman," Miss Dorothy cooed.

"Yes, I am very lucky," Millie agreed.

Alone in her room, Millie stood by her window and gazed out at the city lights and the stars overhead. She was lucky to have found Mr. Graydon, but would she be smart enough to land him? And yet somehow the thought of a victory did not fill her with the elation she thought she should feel.

In a big city like New York, a person ought to be able to sell an awful lot of paper clips . . . but that was a dead-end road: she was never going to see Jimmy Smith again!

## Chapter Nine

The next morning Millie sat solemnly waiting for Mr. Graydon to give her dictation, but Mr. Graydon's mind was elsewhere. "That Miss Dorothy," he said in a voice of exquisite agony. "Oh, great Scott, that Miss Dorothy! Pretty as a peach, and skin to beat the band. A perfect little pippin."

"Perfect," Millie agreed, her eyes downcast and her voice subdued.

"What a dandy little bundle for a fellow to cuddle." Trevor Graydon's eyes were beholding a vision in his mind.

"Yes. Dandy." Millie stood up, her heart sinking into dejection.

"Imagine all that sweet softness in your arms . . ."

Millie walked to the door. She could not bear to hear any more. In a choked voice that she tried to make sound normal, she said, "I'll type up this survey report right away, Mr. Graydon. Original and five."

"Don't forget the dinner reservation at the Plaza," he

reminded her. "The Candle Nook Room. A quiet corner table for two. I think Miss Dorothy's for the Plaza, don't you?"

"Among other things—yes," Millie stated in a flat tone.

"And the flowers." Trevor Graydon was going all out.

"There's a florist just around the corner from the hotel. I'll order from them." Always the secretary but never the bride, she thought to herself morosely. The cruelty of life: to order flowers for another girl.

"That's using the old bean, John." Trevor Graydon was jovial. "Roses. Pink. Plump. Long stemmed. Two dozen in a vase."

Crestfallen, Millie walked out the door into her own office. So that's the way it was. All of her dreams shattered. But I'll be brave, she thought, resolutely picking up the telephone and asking for the Hotel Plaza. "Candle Nook Room. Mr. Trevor Graydon would like a quiet corner for two. Tonight. Seven-thirty." She hung up the phone and looked around the room disconsolately. This was the end. She gave the golf club standing near her desk a little kick and rubbed the sore muscles of her arms. All that swinging for nothing. How could golf have hoped to stand a chance against a peaches-and-cream complexion and golden curls?

With a heavy heart Millie picked up the phone a second time and ordered the flowers.

But she must not wallow in self-pity, Millie thought sternly. She must be plucky and brave. She must face the world as it really was and carry on.

Resolutely she spread out her handkerchief on her desk, and took her few belongings out of the drawer: her lipstick, rouge, the tiny bottle of perfume and her package of cigarettes. Sadly she wrapped them up in the handkerchief. But the sight was too pitiful. Hurriedly Millie ran out of the office to the sanctuary of the ladies' room, where she could cry in peace.

To start all over again seemed like too much, but go on with her quest she must. She would say a dignified farewell to Mr. Trevor Graydon and start tramping the streets once again in search of the job with the boss who would be Mr. Right.

Millie dried her eyes and went back to the office to face her capricious destiny. Absent-mindedly she noticed a man, strapped in a belt, sitting outside her twentieth-story window, washing it. There was a gentle tap on the window that made her look a second time.

To her startled amazement, the face grinning at her through the glass was none other than that belonging to Jimmy Smith. Millie was across the room in a flash. "Jimmy! You crazy kid! What in the world are you doing? Get in here!" Frantically she worked at opening the big window, and when she finally did manage to push it up, almost knocked Jimmy out of his belt.

"Get in here." She had him by the arm. Millie peered down the twenty floors to the street and came as near to fainting as she ever had in her life.

She sank down on the floor in a heap of exhaustion. In a minute Jimmy was beside her, sitting very close.

"You all right?" he asked solicitously.

"Am *I* all right? You scared me near to death. What were you doing out there?"

"The dame in the front office said you never wanted to see me again."

"Well, I did say that, Jimmy . . ." She looked up into his eyes. "But you are my friend after all, I guess . . . and I am glad to see you. I was feeling awful blue."

"You're a strange little bird, Millie," Jimmy said, leaning closer to her.

"You look different," Millie said, examining his face.

"I lost my glasses."

"You have nice eyes," Millie said, looking straight into them.

Jimmy batted his eyes exaggeratedly. "You should catch them by candlelight. Have dinner with me?"

"Well . . . all right. But Dutch treat. At the automat. I'm quitting my job. Mr. Graydon isn't available any more."

Jimmy was jubilant. "Oh, boy, that's corking!"

"He's lost his heart to . . . to a friend of ours," Millie said mournfully.

"Miss Dorothy?"

Millie was aghast. "How did you guess?"

"Who else do we both know? Unless it's Muzzy."

"Don't be bitter, Jimmy," Millie said sympathetically. "Don't blame Miss Dorothy. I *really* don't. Or Mr. Graydon either. Love swamped them. We're too young to live a life of hate."

"You're the one who should be on the stage," Jimmy said, laughing. "You're good."

Millie stared at him incredulously. "But you don't seem to care that Miss Dorothy has fallen for Mr. Graydon."

"I don't," Jimmy said shrugging.

Millie was shocked. "How fickle can you be!" She was truly amazed by Jimmy's casual attitude, and it gave her no comfort to think of him flitting from one girl to another.

"John!" Trevor Graydon's voice interrupted their conversation.

"Your *ex*-lover," Jimmy said, standing up.

"Coming, Mr. Graydon," Millie called out, giving Jimmy a venomous glance.

"Don't look at me that way." Jimmy gave her a kiss on the tip of her nose. "Pick you up at seven. And we are not dining Dutch treat at the automat. I am taking you to an elegant restaurant and you are going to have the best-fed picnic you ever put to your bee-stung lips. Lobster. Steak. Cherries jubilee. Nothing but the best for my date, by jingo!"

When Millie walked home from the subway that evening, impulsively she stopped at the corner florist and bought herself a small bunch of sweet peas to wear that night. Mentally she thumbed her nose at the long-stemmed red roses in a vase: all right for Trevor Graydon . . . he could have his little table at the Plaza and his pippin with the golden curls . . . the stars would still shine and the moon would still rise. Millie had a friend and her own life to lead. The sweet peas would look exactly right on her new violet crepe de Chine gown.

As Millie was about to go into her room, Mrs. Meers emerged from Miss Dorothy's room with a spray gun in her hand, wearing a surgeon's mask tied across her nose and mouth. "For heaven's sake! What's the matter now?" Millie asked in astonishment.

"Have to keep the old place clean," Mrs. Meers said cheerfully. "Marvelous stuff, does a wonderful job. But my nostrils are very delicate, very sensitive. Cheerio, Millie dear." She glided past Millie with triumphant eyes exuding a faint musty and lethal odor. Playfully she pointed the spray gun at Millie, and a very tiny amount of whatever was in it came out. In dismay Millie watched the sweet peas in her hand wilt. "Powerful stuff," Mrs. Meers muttered apologetically. "It does a thorough job, a clean sweep. Guaranteed to get anything that crawls . . ."

"What was crawling in Miss Dorothy's room?" Millie asked in horror.

But Mrs. Meers was already in the elevator and did not answer.

Woefully Millie threw the dead sweet peas into the wastebasket and felt it was an ill omen for the evening ahead. Her spirits brightened when she put on her new dress (bought, she had to admit a bit sadly, with Trevor Graydon in mind), brushed her hair, hung her beads around her neck, and fastened some long, dangling earrings to her ears. She was ready to cope with whatever still unexplored regions of platonic friendship might be discovered in the course of an evening.

She was ready and waiting when Jimmy came to pick her up, and seeing his ready smile set off by a stunning blue shirt and a bow tie, she wondered exactly what Mr. Plato had had in mind when he set up the rules for his famous friendship between the sexes.

True to his word, Jimmy took her to an elegant restaurant on Park Avenue and bought her the best dinner on the menu. Millie sat back in her chair luxuriating in the soft lights, the gleaming silver and white damask cloths, the fashionable people at the other tables. This was truly living, in a style to which she intended to become accustomed. But Millie's practical mind could not stop its wheels from turning round.

"You're going to have to sell an awful lot of paper clips to pay for this," Millie said.

"Don't worry, my little peach," Jimmy said grandly. "Do not trouble your pretty little head about such mundane matters."

However, when the waiter presented the bill to Jimmy, Millie excused herself to go to the ladies' room. She could not bear to be witness to the enormous wad of money Jimmy was going to have to leave in exchange for one meal already consumed.

When Millie emerged from the ladies' "lounge," as it was daintily called, freshly powdered, lipsticked and rouged, there was no Jimmy in sight. Millie's misgivings assaulted her anew when the headwaiter took her arm and briskly escorted her to the back of the restaurant, where the smells from the kitchen were unmistakable.

In a few moments Millie was standing beside Jimmy, a large apron wrapped around her best dress, bathed in stony silence, drying the dishes that he was washing.

"The lights have gone out of you," Jimmy said tenderly.

"You pulled the switch, by jingo!" Millie said exploding.

"You don't think having to wash dishes in the most expensive restaurant in New York a lark?" Jimmy's eyes were twinkling.

"You want to know what I think?" Millie spat out the words like so many little bullets in her mouth, building up to tears. "I think we should have gone to the automat. I think it's stealing when a person knows what he has in his pocket and doesn't spend accordingly. I think in his dealings with his girl friends a person should be *honest*. I think you should settle down and work. I think you are the most irresponsible dabbler, playing fancy-free and loose with *everyone*. Living moment to moment. Never getting involved. Throwing yourself away. Burning yourself up when you could be something." Her eyes were brimming.

"All right, all right. Call Miss Dorothy at the Candle Nook Room. Ask her to come and bail us out."

Millie was aghast. "I'll do no such thing."

"She has the money," Jimmy said. "She's rich, very rich, isn't she?"

"A fortune hunter to boot," Millie stated flatly.

"I'll pay her back," Jimmy said.

"How, in paper clips?" Millie put a dish on the counter with a thud.

"Well, I'm going to call her," Jimmy said firmly. "You're not having a lark. You got a nickel?"

"No," Millie said haughtily, and turning around almost collided with a waiter on the run with a trayful of dirty cups and saucers. "Hey, honey, the coffee klatch in back's runnin' low on cups," he shouted to Millie. "Tote 'm that tray and make it snappy. Hop, hop."

Completely intimidated and not knowing what else to do, Millie grabbed up the tray of clean cups and hurried off in her apron. "No, not the restaurant, honey," the waiter called her hastily. The *back* room. That way." He indicated an unobtrusive steel door leading from the kitchen.

Millie pushed her way through, balancing the loaded tray carefully, and found herself in a small, wood-paneled room filled with people and smoke. The room was dark, lit only by candles, and Millie could barely make out the faces of the well dressed diners, who, judging from the noise and the boisterous laughter, seemed to be having one heck of a time. A girl tinkling at a piano and singing the blues added to the party atmosphere.

A husky man, stuffed into a too-small tuxedo, stood near the door and motioned to a service stand where he told Millie to put down her tray. Relieved of her burden, Millie was able to take a good look around the room. The only thing on the tables were coffee cups, but everyone sure seemed to be having a very jolly time—except one lone man sitting by himself in a booth. He had his coffee cup between both hands in front of his face. When he put the cup down, Millie had a shock.

The sad-sack man was none other than Trevor Graydon. Millie hurried over to him. "Good evening, Mr. Graydon. I thought you were at the Candle Nook Room."

Mr. Graydon looked up in bewilderment. He seemed somewhat disheveled, and his speech was a little thick. It took him a second or two to focus on Millie. "She stood me up," he said in misery. "I went to the Priscilla to call for her. The lady at the desk said she checked out. No note, no nothing. No forwarding address. John, where is she?" He turned a pitiful face to Millie.

Millie was stunned. "I don't know. How very strange." Mr. Graydon drained his cup and set it down with a big sigh. "Just like that, she left," he said.

"Let me get you some more coffee," Millie said compassionately, picking up his cup. The whisky fumes from the cup hit her.

"Strong spirits!" Millie said sternly.

"Not strong enough," Mr. Graydon wailed.

"Now you stop this." She tried to get him up. "You'll upset that lovely system of yours. Come meet Jimmy." She tugged at his arm. "Maybe he can figure it out."

"Dear Miss Dorothy," Millie murmured half to herself, "why would she slip away like that?"

Back in the kitchen Millie told Jimmy what had happened. He was visibly upset. "It doesn't seem possible," he said. "Dorothy wouldn't just leave without telling anyone her plans. And I spoke to her late this afternoon."

"So did I," Millie said.

"Damn! I'm sorry, Millie. But something's up." Millie found herself feeling sorry for Jimmy now too, as well as for Mr. Graydon. He may be a rounder, she thought, but he really does care for her. Millie looked from one man to the other. "What should we do?" she asked.

"Something's not right," Jimmy insisted.

"You suspect foul play?" Trevor Graydon asked, sobered by now.

"I don't know. Could you come up with the jack to spring us from this kitchen, Mr. Graydon?"

Trevor Graydon reached for his wallet. "Good as done, boy."

"I want to get right over there and search her room. Mrs. Meers isn't telling the whole story."

In a few minutes the three of them were out of the restaurant and in a taxi headed for the Hotel Priscilla.

## Chapter Ten

Mrs. Meers was sitting at her desk when Millie and the two young men came in. Trevor Graydon explained the situation. "Surely she left a note or something," Mr. Graydon insisted.

Mrs. Meers was one-hundred percent charm. She was obviously taken with Trevor Graydon's correct good looks, and kept making eyes at him. "No, sir. I told you all I know. Miss Brown checked out a little after seven this evening. She left nothing."

Trevor Graydon was baffled. "But my appointment with her was important . . . I thought."

"I am so sorry." She spoke with an air of weary sophistication. "Here we see so much of this. *Young* girls are so skittish—so undependable. They often take it into their heads to suddenly run home to mama."

"She was an orphan," Mr. Graydon stated flatly.

"Or slip into oblivion," Mrs. Meers went on glibly, "possibly with some forbidden love her friends knew nothing about . . ."

"I think," Trevor Graydon spoke in a steely voice, "I had best call the police in on this. A well-bred young lady like Miss Brown certainly would have at least left a thank-you note for the flowers I sent her."

Mrs. Meers widened her long, narrow eyes. "True . . ." she hesitated for a second or two. "Oh, I wasn't on the desk at the time she left, sir," she continued more smoothly. "Let me check once again for you, excuse me." She started for the back office.

"Oh, I'm sure you searched thoroughly. And I did want to talk to you about–"

"The young clerk is so careless." Mrs. Meers was on her way. "A letter could be anywhere. No one takes pride in their work anymore." She opened the door and closed it quickly behind her, but Millie had a glimpse of the two Chinese laundrymen sitting at a table with their heads bent over a Mah Jong board.

"Mrs. Meers is so hospitable," Millie murmured, "fancy her entertaining the laundrymen . . ." Jimmy and Mr. Graydon were too absorbed in the problem of Miss Dorothy to pay any attention to an observation on Mrs. Meers' finer qualities. They waited for her to return impatiently.

"There is nothing," Mrs. Meers told them graciously a few moments later. "I searched high and low. High and low," she added with a mysterious little giggle.

"We would like to see her room, if you don't mind," Jimmy said.

Mrs. Meers looked offended. "My dear young man, there's nothing in her room. I told you she checked out. Besides," Mrs. Meers added with her devastating barracuda smile, "we can't allow any males upstairs. Naughty, naughty," she said shaking her finger coyly in front of Jimmy's upturned nose.

The three of them turned away disconsolate. "Let's get organized and figure this out," Trevor Graydon said crisply, outside the hotel. Millie led them to a coffee shop around the corner. She wished, modestly, that she were someone like Joan of Arc, and that she could selflessly lead this small battalion of two men to the woman they loved. Let them fight it out then, she thought, and may the best man win. As for herself, she would bravely hide her own sorrow in solitude . . .

"Is there a fire escape to that hotel?" Jimmy asked, breaking into her thoughts of martyrdom.

"Yes, there is. It leads into the back hall," Millie told him.

"By jingo! That's it. I will get into Miss Dorothy's room." Over the coffee cups, the three of them put their heads together to plot their campaign.

A short while later Millie was crouched beside an open window in the back hall, waiting for Jimmy to make the climb up the fire escape to the twelfth floor. She helped him over the sill when he finally appeared. Together they tiptoed down the hall to Miss Dorothy's room, where, with the aid of a long hairpin, Jimmy was able to unlock the door.

"We made it," Millie said with relief, inside the room. Jimmy switched on the lights, and they both immediately saw the pink roses on the night stand.

"And there's her checkbook," Millie cried, spying it lying on the desk. "She can't be too far."

Jimmy opened the closet door. "All her clothes are here! Suitcases, shoes, suits . . . and she's supposed to have checked out without a word? A girl just doesn't do that."

"Ethel Pease did," Millie said with a flash of memory. "And Fanny did . . . and another girl when I first moved in. All of them here one day, gone the next, without a word to anyone . . . except Mrs. Meers . . ."

Suddenly they both froze as they heard a sound coming down the hall. It was the familiar squeak, squeak of the laundry basket, and then Mrs. Meer's muffled voice whispering in Chinese.

"Drat! Mr. Graydon was supposed to keep her occupied downstairs . . . Quick, Millie . . ." Jimmy switched off the lights and pushed Millie under the bed, snuggling in beside her just in time to hear the key turn in the lock. "This is kinda nice," Jimmy murmured, getting as close to Millie as possible.

"Jimmy!" Millie reprimanded him sharply, and moved away from him. "Never serious," she said in a whisper.

From their hiding place under the bed they saw the lights go on, and the feet of Mrs. Meers and the slippered feet of the two Chinese men come into the room, the Chinese pushing the laundry basket. Mrs. Meers gave out some sharp orders in Chinese. Terrified, Millie crept back close to Jimmy's side. Peering out, wide-eyed, they watched the men empty the closet and dump Miss Dorothy's clothes into the laundry basket. After giving the room a final survey, Mrs. Meers yanked the pink roses out of their vase and stuffed them, blooms down, into a wastebasket by the bed at Jimmy's head.

Jimmy sniffed the roses and had to stifle a cough. He sniffed again, and then shook his head vigorously to clear it, and pushed himself and Millie away from the wastebasket. Practically holding their breath, they waited for Mrs. Meers, the two men and the laundry basket to shuffle across the room, and sighed with relief when the lights were switched off and they heard the click of the lock in the door close behind the sinister trio.

"Oh, Jimmy. What'll we do?" Millie asked in alarm, crawling out from under the bed.

Jimmy wiped some of the large areas of dust off Millie's dress and his trousers. "Something fearful is happening. Those roses are *doped*."

Millie went to smell them for herself, but Jimmy yanked her away. "Don't go near them."

"Why they smell like Mrs. Meers' cleaning fluid," Millie exclaimed in wonder. "Just like the stuff she has in her spray gun."

Jimmy grabbed Millie by the arm. "You've seen her use it?"

"Why yes. She sprayed this very room."

"Oh, my goodness!" Jimmy moaned.

Quickly they agreed that Jimmy would exit by the

fire escape and meet Millie and Trevor Graydon in the all-night coffee shop.

In a short while the three were in a desperate huddle around a table. "You were supposed to keep Mrs. Meers downstairs," Jimmy said accusingly to Mr. Graydon, after having told him what had taken place.

Trevor Graydon was white and shaken. "My gut, my weak gut—you know how it is—I had to leave her alone for a few minutes, and when I came back she was gone."

"You've had a harrowing evening," Millie said sympathetically, "poor dear. Those laundrymen have been following Miss Dorothy," she said thoughtfully. "I realize that now. Remember, Mr. Graydon? Yesterday when you met us in front of the office? The laundry truck parked just up the street!"

"I'm afraid I saw only Miss Dorothy," Trevor Graydon confessed, a dreamy look coming into his eyes.

Jimmy's usual cheerful face was troubled and he was in deep thought. "The Chinese are working for Mrs. Meers. She's got something big going." He turned to Millie. "What do all the missing girls have in common? Money?"

"Oh, no," Millie told him, shaking her head. "Ethel Pease didn't have anything. No family, no friends. Nothing. Neither did Fanny. I forget about what's her name . . . no, she was all alone in the world, too, poor thing. Jimmy, Mrs. Meers is always saying that. She said it to Miss Dorothy when she found out she was an orphan."

"What?" Jimmy asked.

" 'Sad to be all alone in the world.' "

Jimmy and Trevor Graydon exchanged grave looks. "Sad for the victim but very convenient for a vampire like Mrs. Meers," Trevor Graydon said.

"You think that . . ." Jimmy looked at Trevor Graydon over Millie's head.

Mr. Graydon nodded gravely. "I do."

"You don't mean . . ." Jimmy said in consternation.

"I'm afraid I do . . ." Mr. Graydon's face was solemn.

"But by now then, she . . ." Jimmy's unfinished sentence hung in the air.

"Yes," Mr. Graydon said.

"Oh, dear!" Millie had her hands over her mouth.

"Yes, Millie. True but cruel . . . If a girl is all alone in the world and she 'checks out' . . . who's to question her fate?"

"But Miss Dorothy isn't all alone in the world," Jimmy asserted with fervor. "She has us."

Once again they put their heads together to map out their plans.

Before Millie said good night to Jimmy and Trevor Graydon in front of the Priscilla, she slipped upstairs to her room and came down in a few minutes with a small suitcase that she gave to Jimmy. "Everything's in here," she said to him. "Good luck. See you in the morning."

That night before Millie went to sleep she bolted her door tight and pushed her bureau in front of it just to make sure. She wasn't an orphan, but with the mysterious happenings that were going on, you never could tell . . .

The next morning Millie bounced out of bed bright and early but not very much refreshed. Her sleep had been marred by dreams of sinister Chinese men, dark alleys and girls screaming. But there was much to be done, and she got dressed hurriedly. Somewhere in the city Miss Dorothy was in trouble—Miss Dorothy and who knew how many other girls?—and Millie had to help the two men who loved Miss Dorothy find her. The complications of the modern world were awesome.

After gulping down a cup of coffee, Millie joined Trevor Graydon, as had been arranged, and together they got into the red roadster.

A few minutes later they were tailing a cab headed for the Hotel Priscilla. The cab came to a stop in front of the hotel, and Trevor Graydon pulled up the red roadster behind it. Millie had a hard time suppressing a giggle as she watched a figure alight from the cab, and only Mr. Graydon's stern look forced her to control herself.

"But he does look funny," she said apologetically. The object of her laughter was the figure of Jimmy Smith, stylishly dressed in Millie's "fatal" flapper dress and hat, her high heels, gloves and make-up, complete with a triangular beauty spot on his cheek. The cab sped away, and with a surreptitious glance at the occupants of the red roadster, and a little pat on his beauty mark, Jimmy entered the hotel, carrying Millie's suitcase.

"All right, John. Snap to. Let's get organized," Trevor Graydon said tensely.

"Yes sir." Obediently Millie got out of the roadster, and with a little nod to Mr. Graydon, who remained in the car, she nervously went into the hotel. Jimmy was at the desk registering with Mrs. Meers.

"Is there any mail for me, Mrs. Meers?" Millie asked in a stiff voice.

"Too early for mail, you know that Millie," Mrs. Meers told her, busy taking care of her new guest.

"Oh, yes, I forgot . . ." she turned to Jimmy. "Hello. My name's Millie Dillmount."

"Hello." Jimmy spoke in a falsetto voice. "Mine's Mary James . . . I'm new here."

"I hope we'll be friends," Millie said, speaking her rehearsed part well.

"Oh, so do I. I don't know a soul in New York. I don't know a soul anywhere." And speaking directly to Mrs. Meers, he added, "Except back at the orphanage."

Mrs. Meers' face lit up, and her sharp-toothed smile came on. "Sad to be all alone in the world, poor dear," she said, handing Jimmy a key. "Twelfth floor dear."

"I'll show him the way," Millie offered, leading Jimmy to the elevator. As they were standing waiting for the slow, rickety elevator to come down, Millie noticed Mrs. Meers staring out of the hotel entrance, and she realized that she was looking at Trevor Graydon, sitting in the roadster outside. She must like his looks too, Millie thought . . . he gets them all. Then Mrs. Meers stood up and walked outside, pulling one of her long hairpins out of her hair. Millie wondered what Mrs. Meers was up to now, the old fox . . . but the elevator came along and Millie couldn't see. But Trevor Graydon's no orphan, and he can take care of himself, Millie reasoned, putting Mrs. Meers from her mind for the moment.

She was in fact absorbed in watching Jimmy's performance as he smiled sedately to the other girls in the elevator. He should have been an actor, Millie thought, admiringly; if we ever find Miss Dorothy, they'd make a marvelous team. The idea made her sigh.

At the twelfth floor they got out together with some of the other girls.

"Thank you, miss," Jimmy said pointedly to Millie in front of the door to his room. "I'll be seeing you."

"Yes, fine." Millie went into her own room and closed the door.

She wondered why she wasn't tired. It had been a hectic night and a wild morning, but the excitement of it kept her going. She also hadn't had time to think about herself and the unhappy fact that the two eligible men in her life were both in hot pursuit after the missing girl. Which one would win, she wondered?

## *Chapter Eleven*

After washing her face and refreshing herself, Millie opened her door to cross the hall to confer with Jimmy. She was stopped, however, by seeing a rather gorgeous, big-busted girl, knocking on Jimmy's door. What was that fickle boy up to now? Couldn't he keep his mind even now on the business at hand . . .

Millie was too curious to close her door completely, so she kept it open a crack to peek. Jimmy opened his door to the girl's voice, "Is Miss Dorothy here?"

"No, sorry. She's moved," Jimmy said, moving from one foot to the other on his high heels.

"Gee, too bad." The girl expanded her chest practically in Jimmy's face, much to Millie's disgust. "I wanted to show her how they turned out," the girl said.

"Apparently just splendid," Jimmy said admiringly.

"Not bad."

"No . . . no, I'd say not bad at all."

"Not stylish, I know." She leaned closer to Jimmy.

"But Dickie, my new flame, likes jazz babies with fronts. As soon as the cluck proposes, out comes the cotton."

"Cotton?" Jimmy was shattered.

"Honey, I'm as flat as Dickie. I can't wait to see his face on our wedding night when most of me goes into the top bureau drawer . . . we girls have to be smart these days. Well, see you in the shower . . ." and off she went, leaving a disillusioned Jimmy behind.

Millie stuck her head out of her door. "Millie, you don't have any surprises for the top bureau drawer, do you?"

Millie gave him her innocent, dazzling smile, but did not commit herself, although she was rather glad that none of the new type bras had succeeded in flattening her out. She was just about to run across to Jimmy's room when Mrs. Meers came down the hall. Millie quickly ducked behind her door, but gave herself a peep opening again.

Jimmy greeted Mrs. Meers in his falsetto voice, although the strain of the high heels was beginning to tell as he moved uneasily from one foot to the other. "I have something for you dear," Mrs. Meers said, displaying a large, round button, edged with red ribbon, with the name *Mary* printed in its center. "I make them up myself for our new girls—especially the lonely ones. It's a little welcome present. Here, let me pin it on you right now." She put the pin high up on Jimmy's shoulder, as close to his nose as she could get it. Jimmy sniffed an unpleasant odor emanating from the pin. He winked at Millie, whose eyes were peering from behind the crack in her slightly open door.

"I'll just check and see that everything's all right," Mrs. Meers said, walking into Jimmy's room. "Stationery, envelopes . . . I'll make sure there's ink . . ."

"What's she doing in your room?" Millie whispered to Jimmy, who was fussing with the big button, trying to figure out where the smell came from.

"I dunno . . . just checking," she said.

"You'd better keep an eye on the old fox," Millie warned.

Jimmy turned around in time to see Mrs. Meers closing the ink well, but too late to know that she had dropped a small pellet into it.

"Everything's just fine and dandy in here," Mrs. Meers said to Jimmy with a benign expression on her face. "I'll leave you, dear, so you can relax . . ."

"It's very kind of you. I can't wait to get acquainted, not having any friends or folks, like I told you," Jimmy said.

"We'll take good care of you—you won't be lonesome for long." She gave a little laugh and sailed out of the room.

As soon as Mrs. Meers' back was turned, Jimmy ducked into Millie's room, unpinning the button. They both examined it, and Jimmy found a tiny open vial of liquid hidden in the folds of the ribbon. "Aha," he cried with delight. "We've foiled her this time." Hastily he emptied the vial down Millie's sink.

Millie was shocked. "But she was so nice all the time. She worked so hard . . ."

"She's working every minute. Never stops. You're a sweet, innocent girl, Millie," he said, looking into her eyes, "and you don't know how much evil there is in this world."

"I don't want to know either," she said, suddenly embarrassed at having Jimmy in her room even though he was dressed as a girl. It didn't seem right.

Jimmy sensed her shyness. "Got to take these darn shoes off," he said gruffly. "Don't know how you girls manage. See you in a few minutes . . ."

"Don't take any wooden nickels," Millie said affectionately. Alone in her room, Millie went to the window and leaned out to see if Mr. Graydon was still there in the roadster. He was sitting with his pipe in his hand like a stone statue. She yoo-hooed to him, but got no response. She then let out a loud whistle, and called out, "Hey, Mr. Graydon . . ." But he didn't move. She decided she'd better get Jimmy. He could undoubtedly yell or whistle louder than she.

She was stopped at the door, however, by the big-busted girl, who was now in a robe on her way to the shower. "Hi, kiddo." The girl stopped Millie. "I was telling your new friend across the way about my boy friend Dickie. He's a healthy young animal. But he can be a gentleman. So I said to him, 'You're on your honor with a lady'; and he said nuts, he was going to take a kiss anyway; and I said, 'Take a kiss, you'll lose a lip.' "

"Ha ha, that's pretty good." Millie laughed appreciatively, and made a move to cross the hall, but the girl kept on talking.

"So I pecked him pertly on the cheek, said 'See you in church,' and turned on the lights. He got the point. Well, see you in the shower," and she ambled her way down the hall.

Millie dashed into Jimmy's room, and was alarmed to find him slumped over the desk. She ran over to him and shook him gently, trying to rouse him, but he was lifeless.

"Oh, dear, oh dear . . ."

Millie didn't know what to do. Her heart was hammering nervously. She ran to Jimmy's window and saw Trevor Graydon still sitting stonelike in the same position. She came back to Jimmy, and then spied a note on the desk. She picked it up and read: "Dear Millie. I am going to *pretend* to be doped so Mrs. Meers will 'check me out' and lead us to Miss Dorothy. Thought I ought to let you know, to avoid any Romeo-Juliet kind of mix-up. You see, I love Yo . . ." The ink trailed away into a faint line.

Joyously Millie hugged Jimmy's limp neck. "And I love you, you funny mutt," she cried. And then she took another look at his face and listened to his puffy, rhythmic breathing. "Jimmy? Jimmy . . . You're *not* pretending! Oh dear, oh dear . . ." She ran to the window again. "Psst . . . psst . . . Mr. Graydon . . ." This time the familiar laundry truck, with its back doors open, was parked directly in front of the hotel. But there was still no response from Trevor Graydon. Frantically Millie rapped on the window and whistled again. "Mr. Graydon, *please* answer me, Mr. Graydon . . ." The street noises came up to her, but Mr. Graydon did not make a sound or budge from his position.

Then Millie heard a new noise: the squeak, squeak of the laundry basket coming down the hall. She ran from the window back to Jimmy at the desk, and tried desperately to lift him, but he was far too heavy for her. Her heart froze at a sinister knock on the door. In a flash Millie grabbed Jimmy's note and darted under the bed. She scrambled under just in time, because Mrs. Meers entered briskly, followed by the two Chinese men pushing the laundry basket.

Mrs. Meers walked over to Jimmy, crumpled up at the desk, lifted his head and peered at his face with some contempt. "Not much," she said jauntily, "but in a dark corner on the late, late shift . . ." She gave a macabre laugh and stalked out of the room.

With her heart pounding so loudly Millie was afraid the Chinese would hear it, she watched them stuff poor limp Jimmy into the laundry basket, and saw their slippered feet patter across the room, pushing Jimmy out with them.

The minute the door closed behind them, Millie flew over to the window and leaned far out. "Mr. Graydon," she called. "They've got Jimmy in the laundry basket. Mr. Graydon, the laundrymen . . ."

But Mr. Graydon was stony. Millie screamed and rapped on the window to no avail. She ran down the hall to the elevator, but it had already descended with the Chinese men and their burden. Twelve floors—would it be faster running down or waiting for the darn slow elevator to come up again? Millie ran down the stairs to the eleventh floor, then to the tenth, then to the ninth, and had to stop exhausted to catch her breath. Then she rang for the elevator. Her heart was thumping to each creaking noise as the elevator made its interminably slow way up; finally it arrived and she got in and tapped her foot nervously as it shuddered and quaked all the way down. Millie sent a prayer up to heaven: please don't get stuck. At last the lobby.

Millie was across the hall in about half a second and out the door just in time to see the doors on the back of the parked laundry truck close, with the laundry basket inside. She jumped into the little red roadster beside Mr. Graydon. "Oh, Mr. Graydon, quick, let's follow that truck. Act natural, but please, let's not lose it. They've got Jimmy inside . . ."

The pipe in Trevor Graydon's hand did not move. The laundry truck pulled away. "Oh, Mr. Graydon, please, we're not playing statues . . . they're getting away," she screamed, "and they're taking Jimmy with them." Frantically she turned around and shook Mr. Graydon, and to her horror he fell forward like a log and slumped over the steering wheel, with which the horn started blaring shrill and steadily.

Millie was beside herself. "Oh, Mr. Graydon . . . oh my, Jimmy . . . holy smoke!" She discovered a tiny dart sticking into Mr. Graydon's neck just above his Arrow collar. "Oh, that woman!" Millie remembered the way Mrs. Meers had been staring at Trevor Graydon earlier. "She will stop at nothing to achieve her dastardly aim," Millie said to the unresponsive hunk of man beside her. Down the street she could see the laundry truck stopping for a red light. "There's only one thing to do," Millie said with determination, getting some small comfort out of pretending Trevor Graydon could hear her: it made her feel less alone. She got out of the roadster and ran around to the driver's side. With all her strength, she pushed Mr. Graydon to the other side and slipped into the driver's seat herself.

"Oh, dear, now what?" Scared stiff, Millie stared at the array of mechanical instruments before her. "What do I do? That's the starter . . . that's the gas, I think . . . and that's the brake, I hope . . ."

Tentatively she pushed a few things, and out of the corner of her eye she spied Mrs. Meers come dashing through the revolving doors of the hotel. Mrs. Meers was wild-eyed, some of her hair loose from its hairpins, and Millie could hear her screeching loudly, "Taxi . . . Taxi . . . for heaven's sake, a taxi . . ."

Millie pushed something that sent the car forward with a lurch, and it went careening down the street. She held on to the steering wheel for dear life. Behind her Millie could still hear Mrs. Meers screaming, "Taxi . . . oh, this town. You never can find a cab when you need one . . ."

The laundry truck was about three blocks ahead of her. "Keep your eye on the ball," Millie said to the limp body beside her, torn between keeping a watch on the laundry truck and trying desperately to avoid the rush of the traffic around her. "Oh, dear . . ." She missed a taxi by an inch. "Oh, my . . ." It looked as if she were going headlong into an oncoming truck, but the truck driver swerved in time with an oath that made Millie blush. Finally she was safely behind the laundry truck, and she breathed a sigh of relief.

But her ease was not long-lived. She pushed something too hard, and to her disgust the roadster zoomed ahead and left the truck behind her. Millie suddenly realized how exposed she was in the open car, and slouched down in her seat, hoping desperately that the Chinese men would not see her. "That's the *gas*, and *that's* the brake."

There was a faint murmur from the body beside her. "Pretty as a peach . . . skin to beat the band . . . Miss Dorothy . . ."

"He's alive!" Millie cried in delight. The laundry truck was now directly behind her, and in her rear view mirror, Millie could see the two Chinese men eying her. Quickly she grabbed the plaid blanket from across the back of the seat and hurriedly covered Trevor Graydon with it. The stop light changed, and Millie waited for the laundry truck to pass her, ducking her head as it went by, hoping to be invisible.

"Hi there." One of the Chinese men gave her a lascivious leer as they passed by, and Millie returned him a sickly smile. "Nasty old man," she murmured.

"Peaches and cream . . ." murmured Trevor Graydon.

Millie followed as close as she could behind the laundry truck into the narrow, crowded streets of Chinatown. "Their den of iniquity must be down here," Millie said.

"Golden curls to tear a man's heart," Trevor Graydon mumbled.

"Oh dear." Millie and the red roadster were stopped by a Chinese man pushing a handcart across the cobbled street, and the laundry truck disappeared around a corner. What seemed like hours later but was only a few minutes, the red roadster turned the corner on two wheels, and Millie saw the tail end of the laundry truck slide into a narrow alleyway. "Keep your eye on the ball," she said to Trevor Graydon.

"Those eyes, those lips . . ." was his unsatisfactory response.

Weaving the car in and out, Millie made her way down the cluttered street lined with wagons of strange-looking produce, carts, trucks and boys on bicycles. Finally Millie saw the laundry truck parked beside a three-story red brick building. With a sudden swerve of the steering wheel, Millie careened the roadster into the alleyway, and pulled to a stop behind the laundry truck. The back of the truck was open, and the inside of it was empty.

They had disappeared, the two Chinese men, the laundry basket and Jimmy inside of it.

Millie stood staring into the empty truck dumbfounded. She looked up at the sky. Had they taken off in a balloon? There was no sign of life anywhere in the alley. The red brick wall of the building was as silent as a tombstone. Only Trevor Graydon's heavy breathing as he stuck his head out from under the blanket broke the stillness.

"Jimmy . . . Jimmy . . ." Millie's sad voice called out into the void, and her plaintive voice came back to her in a faint echo.

Millie ran up and down the alley, calling Jimmy's name, and then went back to the street. "They must be here some place!" Nervously she peered into the strange shops and buildings. "Ugh . . ." Millie pulled her nose out of a store filled with raw fish and odd vegetables; then there was a tourist shop filled with tea sets, beads and incense burning; meat stores, shops filled with exotic kimonos, jewelry, pastries. She ran from one to the other, eying the solemn shopkeepers, who paid no attention to her. But her two Chinese men, and their precious laundry basket were nowhere in sight.

She ran into an ancient fortune-cookie factory and looked at two women, who ignored her. One was pecking away with one finger on a long, narrow strip of paper in a typewriter. Millie saw her cut off a strip and hand it to her friend, who laughed hysterically and stuffed the paper into a cookie. "And I always believed what they said," Millie murmured. "Oh, dear, nothing is what it seems. Who can a girl trust? The whole world is topsy-turvy!"

Millie ran on frantically. "Has anyone seen two Chinese men with a laundry basket?" she asked the Chinese women on the street, and they stared at her with hurt eyes.

Finally Millie ran back to the red roadster parked in the alleyway. Trevor Graydon was curled up under the blanket sound asleep. Despondently she walked back to the entrance to the alley and again looked up and down the street. Her attention was caught by a beautiful Chinese girl who stepped out on to a balcony and was staring at Millie intently from large, dark, almond-shaped eyes. Another girl joined her, and the two pointed at Millie and were looking at her suspiciously.

Millie was terrified. She retreated back into the alley and leaned against the brick wall, breathing unevenly. Danger lurked in every corner, sinister eyes were staring at her from every crevice.

Nervously she went further along the wall until she saw an open window above her that she hadn't noticed before; but it was over her head and she couldn't see into it, even if she dared to look. She leaned against the wall, still feeling the girls' eyes upon her, and, trying to look nonchalant, took out her battered but unopened package of cigarettes, pulled one out and lit it. Her first puff choked her into a fit of coughing and brought tears to her eyes. "I can't even pretend to be a sophisticate," she thought in desperation and threw her lit cigarette, and the package after it, over her head. They both sailed into the open window of the red brick building.

## Chapter Twelve

Millie's lit cigarette sailed right past a weather-beaten sign on the side of the red brick building that said "WOO FIREWORKS FACTORY."

Millie leaned back against the red brick wall and suddenly a magnificent skyrocket came shooting out over her head. Then another and another. A hidden door in the brick wall opened and a stream of Chinese businessmen came out amidst a cloud of fantastic pinwheels, smoke bombs and multicolored Roman candles. Millie ran to the far side of the building at the back of the alley, and here workingmen were tumbling out of windows, shouting and screaming.

"Help, help!" Millie heard a feminine voice above her, and she looked up at a second-story window and caught a glimpse of a head with golden curls.

"*Miss Dorothy!*" Millie's heart surged with joy. Battling her way against the onrush of Chinese men coming out of the building, Millie fought her way inside. It was dark except for the flashing lights of the fireworks, and Millie picked herself a Roman candle to light her way. Holding the candle high above her head, she found steep, narrow rickety stairs with a door at the top. Millie made her way up the stairs, opened the door at the top, and gasped. She faced a sight that turned her flesh to goose pimples and sent shivers up and down her spine.

She was in what obviously had once been a storeroom, dark and dank. It was now lined with crude bamboo jail cells holding a strange cargo: each cell had in it a pretty young girl gagged and bound. Some of the girls were now struggling futilely to get free, while others simply sat on their straw mats staring through the bars in hopeless, frightened despair. On one side of the room there was a row of large boxes, each large enough to hold a girl, with air holes drilled in their sides and carrying large printed labels: "Ship to Mrs. Meers Tea Rooms–Hong Kong," some read. Others said: "Ship to Big Mary's Tart Shop–Peking."

The room was full of smoke. The girls were coughing behind their gags, and even the most lethargic ones were now thrashing around in panic.

"Oh dear, oh dear!" Millie flew to the nearest cell, where a lovely blonde was imploring her with her eyes. Millie tore at the bindings on the girl's wrists. "It's not a fire," Millie shouted above the din and the commotion of the people still fleeing from the building. "It's not a real fire . . . it's just . . ." And then a gorgeous display of fireworks lit up the room and disappeared out through the small skylight in the ceiling. "It's just fireworks," Millie said. "I hope it'll bring the police." Millie worked frantically at the girl's bindings, biting and yanking at them. While she was doing it, she tried to get some information. "Two Chinese laundrymen with a boy–I mean a girl, a very *tall* girl–did they come in? Or a beautiful blonde girl with curls . . . Miss Dorothy?"

The girl grunted and nodded her head, and her melancholy eyes indicated a door at the far end of the musty room.

Millie bit savagely at the last knot. "These Chinese must

have been boy scouts," she mumbled, and then corrected herself hastily. "But boy scouts would never do a thing like this." Finally Millie had the girl's hands freed. The blonde immediately started removing her gag and then her leg ties. "Thank you, oh thank you so much," the girl said. "I'll never forget you."

Millie was already on the run toward the far end of the room. "Untie the others and hide until the police come."

Millie opened a door into a hallway filled with colored smoke. Cautiously she felt her way along the wall. There were many doors and some archways hung with beaded curtains. The smell made by the fireworks was mixed with incense and opium burning. When a firecracker broke through, Millie could see the fine tapestries and Chinese adornments decorating the walls. Millie poked her head into each room and through the beaded curtains. She was shocked by what she saw: each room with its low Chinese bed, its bowl of incense and opium pipe, and exotic kimono draped over the bed. "Oh dear, oh dear me . . . what a wicked world!"

"Miss Dorothy, Miss Dorothy," Millie called out, but each room she went into was empty. In despair she leaned against the wall, rubbing her eyes, which were smarting from the smoke. "I must save her from a fate worse than death," Millie said to herself, thinking with some relief that Jimmy would at least be safe in that respect.

"Oh, Miss Dorothy, where are you?" Millie leaned harder against the wall, and suddenly something clicked, and a hidden panel in the wall slid open. Millie almost fell backwards into a room. It was small and dark like the others, and in it were two beds, each with a figure on it, one in a bundle.

"Oh, Miss Dorothy!" Millie flew over to the one bed and to Miss Dorothy, who looked at her with frightened eyes and a groggy expression. Jimmy was lying on the other bed, still in the laundry bag.

When Miss Dorothy recognized Millie in the darkness, she jumped up and embraced her. The girls hugged each other and both were near tears. "Oh, Millie . . .

Millie, dear Millie . . ." Miss Dorothy hugged her hard.

Millie stood away from her, trying to see Miss Dorothy's face. "Are you all right? They didn't hurt you, did they? I mean . . . they didn't have their way with you?"

"*Really*, Millie!" Miss Dorothy was aghast.

Then Millie spied the little beauty mark that Jimmy had worn now adorning Miss Dorothy's cheek. "How did that get through the laundry bag?" she asked in wonder. "You certainly have a way with you, Miss Dorothy!"

Millie opened the laundry bag and peered at Jimmy, still groggy from the dope. "Quite a fella. Even in his sleep he doesn't miss a trick—or an opportunity. What a man!" she said half in admiration, half in resentment. "Maybe being an orphan has its advantages." For a fleeting second Millie wondered if she had missed something by not being one of the girls abducted, but she hastily put that uneasy thought from her mind.

"I do hope he won't be an addict . . . I mean, after all that dope," Miss Dorothy said.

"Never hurt Sleeping Beauty or Snow White," Millie said in a hard voice. She was still eying the beauty mark on Miss Dorothy's cheek with suspicion and smarting under the strain of having come through fire and smoke to rescue these two. "The little fool from Kansas," Millie muttered. "Come on, let's get out of here. I guess we'll have to carry him." Millie looked down at Jimmy in the laundry bag.

"He was awake for a little while," Miss Dorothy remarked.

"You're telling me!" Millie said in disgust.

Together the girls picked up Jimmy in the laundry bag and staggered down the stairs with him. "He's heavy," Miss Dorothy said, gasping under the load.

"So virile," Millie said with sweet sarcasm.

Outside in the alleyway there was utter confusion. The noisy Chinese workers were milling about, running to and fro with buckets of water. People from the streets had gathered round, and slipping out of the door and running for their lives were the lovely girls from the bamboo jail cells. The blonde Millie had untied spied Millie and ran over and gave her a kiss. "You should get a medal," she said to Millie.

"Yeah, yeah. Think nothing of it," Millie said lightly. "Do it any time."

"Come on," Miss Dorothy said, her eyes frightened among all the Chinese men.

"To the rumble seat," Millie ordered, she and Miss Dorothy picking up the heavy laundry bag again and heading for the red roadster.

There was movement under the plaid blanket when they got to the car. A low voice hummed, "Ah sweet mystery of life . . ."

"Trevor!" Miss Dorothy exclaimed.

"The front seat's taken," Millie said, and shoved Miss Dorothy into the rumble seat, into which the two of them also managed to lift Jimmy.

Millie ran around and got into the driver's seat next to Trevor Graydon. The roadster was surrounded by dozens of Chinese men, some kibitzing, others carrying water buckets. Suddenly Millie saw the two Chinese laundrymen among them and frantically worked at getting the car started. She stepped on the starter, and then on the gas, but she flooded the motor, which sputtered and stopped. "Are you waiting for someone, darling?" Miss Dorothy asked.

Millie gave her a silent but devastating look through the rear mirror.

"I bet you could even make the moon and stars behave," said a mumbled voice from under the blanket.

Miss Dorothy blushed prettily, and Millie gave both the blanket and Miss Dorothy a sour look. "No one around here ever takes time off," Millie said.

Just then a taxi drew up and Mrs. Meers stepped out. She went over to the two Chinese laundrymen and swung them around. Then the three of them headed for the roadster. "Oh, look, there's Mrs. Meers," Miss Dorothy said cheerfully. "Maybe she wants a lift . . ."

Millie saw the three approaching the car, and she got the car started, with a violent jerk, in reverse.

"No, darling, forward . . . forward," Miss Dorothy said helpfully from behind.

Hastily Millie shifted gears, and the roadster spun wildly down the alley, scattering the Chinese and their buckets. In the rear view mirror Millie could see Mrs. Meers and the two Chinese men make for the laundry truck. She also heard police cars come zooming into the alley, their sirens blaring. Millie stepped on the gas, and the car streaked down the street and around a corner.

"Faster, faster!" Miss Dorothy called out gleefully. "It'll go better if you release the brake."

Millie threw her a withering look, but she took the advice. In her mirror she could see the laundry truck behind them.

"It'll be a race to the death—for one of us," Millie cried, exalted. She spun the car around corners, weaved through traffic, passed red lights, but the laundry truck kept close behind.

"Duck!" Millie suddenly screamed out to Miss Dorothy, as she saw Mrs. Meers take aim with an ivory blow gun and a small dart. The dart sailed over Miss Dorothy's head and into the street.

"That was a close one," Millie screamed back to Miss Dorothy. She was beginning to enjoy the excitement of the race. She drove up to the Fifty-Ninth Street Bridge, drove through Long Island City, and sped along Queens Boulevard. There was one haven where she knew they would be safe, and she was heading for it.

"Hey, duck!" Millie called out again as she saw Mrs. Meers getting ready to take aim once more. Millie ducked her head this time too, and again Mrs. Meers missed her shot.

The roadster headed like a homing pigeon for Muzzy's mansion. Miss Dorothy gave her the directions, and by this time Millie took twists and turns like an old pro. "I like this," Millie said, hanging on to the wheel. "There's something to be said for modern inventions."

Finally she saw the walls of the Van Hossmere mansion in the distance, and with one last furious spurt, the roadster made it to the wall and through the gates. The car careened up the driveway and came to an abrupt halt in front of the massive doors.

"We made it," Millie cried, and both she and Miss Dorothy collapsed with relief.

"I didn't know Mrs. Meers was such good friends with the Chinese laundrymen," Miss Dorothy said in surprise.

"You don't know the half of it," Millie told her, explaining how, with her own eyes, she had seen Mrs. Meers kidnapping Jimmy.

"That sweet old thing," Miss Dorothy mused. "You wouldn't believe it."

"You cannot tell a book by its cover," Millie said meaningfully, glancing at Miss Dorothy's curls, and then down at the laundry bag holding Jimmy.

Unexpectedly the huddle under the blanket came to life and Trevor Graydon sat up. "All right now," he said crisply, "let's get organized."

"Righto," Millie said efficiently. "I'll take the head and you take the feet." She pointed to the body in the laundry bag.

"Okay John." Trevor Graydon sprang out of the car, but he took one look at Miss Dorothy, her golden hair glistening in the sunlight, and all his snap left him. His eyes turned dreamy and he started humming again. "Oh, sweet mystery of life . . ."

Miss Dorothy blushed.

"Let's get organized," Millie said. "There's a time and a place for everything."

"Um-mm, yes," Trevor Graydon stammered. He and Millie carried Jimmy into the house, with Miss Dorothy walking daintily behind them.

"Oh, you dears . . ." Muzzy came running to greet them in a toreador costume. "We've been practicing for a bullfight," she said gaily, "but I'm so glad you came. I'm ready to take a rest."

She hugged Millie and Miss Dorothy, and greeted Mr.

Graydon. "Oh, my, what a lot of laundry," she said, looking at the laundry bag.

"It's not laundry. It's Jimmy," Millie said flatly.

"Oh, the poor dear boy. How silly of him to be in a laundry bag." Muzzy bent down and took Jimmy's head in her arms and kissed him.

Millie watched her wide-eyed. "You too?" she asked incredulously.

Jimmy opened his eyes. "Muzzy, darling . . ." he said and nestled in her arms. "By jingo! It's good to see you." He closed his eyes again.

Millie turned her head away. This was too much. "Enough is enough," she murmured, tears choking her throat. "How can a man be so fickle?"

But no one heard her, because Miss Dorothy was batting her lovely eyes at Trevor Graydon, whose face reflected a state of bliss, and Muzzy was embracing a slowly awakening Jimmy, who seemed very happy to be in her well muscled but charming arms.

## *Chapter Thirteen*

"It's nice to be back here," Millie said later that evening as they were all gathered in the tremendous Van Hossmere drawing room. "It's so cosy and homelike."

"It's great to have you here," Muzzy said. She was reclining on a sofa sipping champagne, holding court like a youthful queen mother. She looks like a queen, Millie thought, silently admiring Muzzy's long Grecian chiffon gown, tied at her waist with a golden cord. At least Jimmy has good taste, Millie thought sorrowfully, looking from Muzzy's more mature fascination to Miss Dorothy's dimpled, girlish charms. Miss Dorothy, however, was wholly occupied curled up at Trevor Graydon's feet, holding his free hand. His other hand was holding his pipe as he stood against the mantel, looking down fondly at Miss Dorothy. Every once in a while he extricated his hand from Miss Dorothy's to pat a small strip of adhesive tape on his neck.

Millie, though, was the real center of attraction. She was seated on a plump ottoman, with Jimmy standing proudly over her in a borrowed sweater and slacks. "They always have so many clothes here," Millie had said. "And they fit so well."

"Your adventure sends a chill over my heart," Muzzy was saying. "To think of such ungentlemanly behavior in my beloved New York. Millie, I lift my glass in humble tribute. A miracle, the way you rebuffed those fatheads."

The others all applauded while Millie blushed prettily. "It was nothing . . ." She brushed the whole thing aside with a shrug of her shoulders. "Anyone would do the same."

"You were a brave girl," Muzzy said. "Walking right into their den . . ." Muzzy looked at Miss Dorothy thoughtfully. "I shudder to think of what might have happened . . ."

Trevor Graydon's face paled. "Let us not mention it."

"They would have had a bit of a surprise when they came to me," Jimmy observed. Millie and Miss Dorothy both blushed, but Muzzy laughed out loud. It's her suave sophistication that must capture Jimmy's heart, thought Millie.

Outside the French doors there was a rustle in the bushes. Millie, who was facing the doors, stood up. "I think someone's out there," she said. And then she saw Mrs. Meers ducking behind a bush and the slippered feet of the two Chinese laundrymen slithering behind a tree. In another second a tiny dart flew right past Millie's head, missing her by a fraction of an inch, and landed once again in Trevor Graydon's stiff but ample neck. He froze in his standing position, holding his pipe exactly as he had before.

"Be calm. I'll ring for Mr. Tea," Muzzy said. "He will take care of everything." Languidly Muzzy stretched out her arm and pulled a bell cord. In a few moments Mr. Tea slipped into the room, his solemn eyes noncommittal, and bowed stiffly to everyone.

"Mr. Tea, please take care of some fatheads out in the bushes. They are disturbing us."

Mr. Tea bowed again and slid through the French

doors. "You have wonderful help around here," Millie observed. She turned around and stared at Jimmy meaningfully. "It must be a great place to work—especially if you were a gardener—all that lovely outdoors."

Jimmy smiled back at her, but he didn't say a word.

"Oh, look!" Millie was looking outside again. She saw Mr. Tea face to face with Mrs. Meers, with a gun in his hand. Mrs. Meers and Mr. Tea were bowing to each other. "They're so polite," Millie said, but then she let out a frightened shriek. While Mr. Tea was bowing, Mrs. Meers had given him a sharp knifelike karate blow on the back of his neck. Gracefully, Mr. Tea crumbled to the ground.

"They're coming through the door," Millie screamed, as Mrs. Meers and the two Chinese men did indeed charge through the French doors, with Mr. Tea's gun firmly grasped in Mrs. Meers' right hand.

"Good evening," Mrs. Meers greeted them with her flashing, barracuda smile.

Frightened, Millie ran to Jimmy, while Dorothy took refuge beside stony Trevor Graydon, who did not move a muscle. Jimmy started to make a move toward Mrs. Meers and her two Chinese companions, but Muzzy stopped him with a firm gesture. "Raspberries!" Muzzy cried out with relish.

Muzzy then faced Mrs. Meers, pulling herself up to her full height, and, with a flip gesture, twirling her Grecian skirt, she proceeded to hum a pitch tone, as her singing instructor did, and let go a long, foghorn note. The two Chinese men stopped in their tracks.

"She's obviously mad," Mrs. Meers muttered. "Thin-blooded aristocrats . . ."

Muzzy ignored her and continued hitting descending bass notes that reverberated through the room. One note reverberated right through the lenses of the glasses one of the Chinese men was wearing, and the glass went "Crack, crack!" The bewildered man took off the broken glasses and staggered about blindly.

"*Foo shu, chin chow.*" The other Chinese man advanced toward Muzzy menacingly.

"Yeah, yeah!" Muzzy twisted her shoulder, as her dancing instructor did, and shimmied right up to the Oriental.

"White devil," the man muttered, clearly frightened by this mad woman's gyrations.

"Yeah, yeah!" Muzzy danced around him, getting in some good Charleston kicks in appropriate places, causing the man to clasp his groin with pain.

"*Fu chu.*" He raised his arm as if to destroy Muzzy, but with a firm imitation of Cruncher, she flattened him with a sharp uppercut. "Okay—okay," Muzzy said wiping her hands.

"Get her . . . get the mad thing," Mrs. Meers said to the blinded Chinese man who was still staggering about.

With his arms outstretched he started moving in Muzzy's direction, and Jimmy and Millie ran to her side. With a gay shout, Muzzy picked up the tiny man and threw him to Jimmy and Millie in true bouncing Bernini fashion, leading them in making a human yo-yo of the dazed Chinese man. "*Ecco! Ecco!*" Muzzy cried triumphantly as they wound him up for the finale and sent him sailing out through the French doors.

Muzzy, Millie and Jimmy faced the frantic Mrs. Meers with elaborate bows.

"Mad people . . . mad, thin-blooded aristocrats . . ." Mrs. Meers pointed Mr. Tea's gun at them.

Millie put her hands over her face and turned her head against Jimmy's shoulder. Jimmy put a protecting arm around her. But Muzzy stood alone and laughed at Mrs. Meers.

"Devil . . ." Mrs. Meers took aim directly at Muzzy and fired the gun.

"Oh!" Millie screamed and then opened her eyes to see Mrs. Meers holding a gun in her hand out of the muzzle of which had popped a bright red flag with the word *BANG!* written on it in white. Muzzy was still laughing.

"*Ding foo!*" Mrs. Meers ran for the French doors, with Muzzy after her. As Muzzy ran, she ripped off from around her waist the long golden cord with its heavy gold tassels at each end, and as she followed Mrs. Meers into the garden, she let the gold balls fly like a bola.

"*Ole!*" Muzzy called out, letting the cord wrap itself around the sputtering Mrs. Meers, pinning her arms and legs to her body. "*Ole!*" Muzzy cried. And splash! Mrs. Meers fell headlong like a plank into the pool.

"*Ding foo! Pook, pook, ding foo!*" Mrs. Meers' black head disappeared under the water.

"*Esas son las bolas, Señora,*" Muzzy said with a bow to Mrs. Meers, who was now sitting helpless but upright in the shallow pool, her hair dripping over her anguished face.

"That's that," Muzzy said to Jimmy and Millie when she came back to the living room.

"It pays to have an education," Millie said admiringly to Muzzy.

"I believe one should always keep learning," Muzzy said.

Just then they heard the sound of approaching police sirens. "Ah, my law instructors have arrived," Muzzy said. She went outside to greet the policemen and to ask them to take away Mrs. Meers and her two accomplices.

Millie turned to Jimmy. Miss Dorothy was still snuggled up close to Trevor Graydon, murmuring "My rock."

"Well, I guess I'd better go back to the Hotel Priscilla and start looking for another job tomorrow," Millie said, glancing over at Miss Dorothy and Trevor Graydon. "It's been fun while it lasted." There was a sad note in her voice.

"You can't leave now. It's too late. Muzzy wants us to stay overnight. Besides," Jimmy said, giving her a tender look, "there's something I want to say to you . . ."

Millie looked up at him eagerly. "Yes?"

But before Jimmy could reply, Muzzy came back into the room with a handsome police officer. "This is the heroine, Miss Millie Dillmount," Muzzy said, introducing Millie to the cop. "She'll tell you everything you want to know."

The cop shook Millie's hand vigorously and looked around the room. "What's the matter with him?" he asked, staring at Trevor Graydon's frozen face.

It was then that Millie noticed the little dart in Mr. Graydon's neck. "Oh, he has another one of those things. He's allergic to darts."

Dorothy jumped up, pulled it out and stuck another little piece of adhesive tape on Trevor Graydon's neck. "I love quiet men," Dorothy said.

"You could make the moon and stars behave," Trevor Graydon murmured, the expression on his face barely changing.

"If you don't mind, I'd like to question the little lady alone," the police officer said.

"Righto," Muzzy agreed. "Law and order must be served. Writ of *habeas corpus* means . . ." She took Jimmy on one arm and Miss Dorothy on the other and led them out of the room, explaining the law to them while Trevor Graydon followed on Miss Dorothy's heels.

"I'll tell you everything you want to know," Millie said to the cop and proceeded to tell him all the events from the day when Ethel Pease first disappeared.

"You deserve a medal," the policeman told her when she was finished. "I'll get you a citation from the mayor. We knew there was something fishy going on, but you caught them red-handed. What a dame!"

"I'm a modern," Millie said nonchalantly. "Women don't take a back seat any more."

"You said it, kiddo," the policeman agreed. "I think modern women are great just so long as my wife doesn't get any ideas in her head."

When the policeman left, Millie was alone in the big room. She didn't know where everyone had disappeared to, but since it was late she assumed they had gone to bed. She was tired and depressed. She felt that an episode in her life had ended, and that she was going to have to start all over again with her life in New York, N. Y.

Mr. Tea, his neck in a brace, glided into the room, looked at Millie and glided out again. Millie wondered if she had seen a little smile on his solemn face.

"Well, I guess if everyone else has gone to bed I may as well too," Millie said aloud to the empty room. Listlessly she rang a bell for a maid to show her to her room. Juarez the butler appeared, his smoldering eyes intense in his sleek, swarthy face. "Señorita . . ." He beckoned her to follow him.

He led her through the usual maze of corridors and finally to a huge room with a big four-poster bed. With a bow he left her.

After the excitement of the day, Millie felt very letdown. She got undressed and put on the pair of striped pajamas laid out on the bed for her. Wearily she turned up the sleeves and legs, because they were both too long.

Jimmy . . . Jimmy . . . Her heart was crying out for the fresh, tweedy smell of him . . . But could she give up all her dreams of marrying her boss and settle for paper clips? And could she truly trust Jimmy? Would he always be hugging and kissing some other girl?

Yet, there was the look in his eyes tonight when he'd said "I want to tell you something . . ."

What was the good of being a modern girl, Millie thought, if you didn't act modern? Millie finished rolling up her pajama sleeves and opened the door. "Nothing ventured, nothing gained," her mother back in Kansas used to say.

Millie slipped down the hallway to the room she knew to be Jimmy's. She tapped lightly on the door, but there was no answer. Slowly she eased the door open, and peeked inside. Then Millie froze. Standing in the room, all of them in their pajamas, were Jimmy, Dorothy and Muzzy laughing and hugging each other.

"I didn't think you had them both at the same time," Millie said in an icy, shocked voice.

The three of them faced Millie, Jimmy in the middle

with one arm around Muzzy and the other around Miss Dorothy. "Sure. Wanna join us?" Jimmy asked. "Me and my sister Miss Dorothy," he said, hugging Miss Dorothy, "and my stepmother Muzzy," he added, hugging Muzzy.

"Your stepmother!" Millie was incredulous.

"Yes, even though she is not old enough to be," Jimmy said.

"And your sister! The girl I thought was an orphan without a friend in the world!" Millie stared in disbelief from one to the other. She had to sit down on the bed, the whole idea made her so dizzy. "I've been blind," Millie said, rubbing her eyes. "How foolish of me . . ."

"No, no dear," Muzzy said, stretching out her hands to Millie. "Jimmy is just like his father. He doesn't look much like a *real* multimillionaire to a girl—I was once fooled too."

"You mean you're not in paper clips?" Millie asked in a daze.

"Well, that isn't too far from the truth," Miss Dorothy said. "The fortune was founded in steel . . ."

"But I don't understand. Why? Why?" Millie looked from one to the other.

Muzzy put her arm around Millie. "I know it must be quite a shock, dear. But you see that Judith Tremayne had been sniffing around Jimmy quite a bit, and every fortune hunter in the country was after Dorothy, so I sent the kids out into the real world. I had high hopes they'd find really sweet partners, and they did. They found you and Trevor Graydon. Their father would be so proud of you." Muzzy drew Millie over to stand close to Jimmy.

Jimmy took hold of Millie's hand. Her eyes were still dazed, but they shone when she looked at Jimmy. "I'm first vice president of Van Hossmere World Wide Enterprises," Jimmy said. "Be my stenog?"

Millie shook her head. "Oh, no thank you. I don't want to be your equal any more. I want to be your woman—a dandy little bundle for a fella to cuddle. I'm going back to hoop skirts and flirting fans. You think Miss Dorothy has curls? Wait."

Jimmy gave her a hug for an answer, and then a kiss full on her lips. "By jingo, you're just the right little bundle for me!" he said. Millie did not disagree.

The next morning at breakfast Millie and Jimmy, Dorothy and Trevor Graydon and Muzzy were served by Mr. Tea. "What do you think, Tea?" Jimmy asked, looking at Millie with tender eyes.

"I have been watching her most close. I approve. A good old-fashioned girl," Mr. Tea declared with solemn dignity.

Millie laughed. "And I thought I was frightfully modern."

"A rose is a rose," Jimmy said, bending over and kissing her. "What would you like for a wedding present, Mrs. Van Hossmere?"

"A checkbook, by jingo!" Millie said promptly. "Rich people can nickel-and-dime you to death."

"I think," Muzzy said thoughtfully, "we could have a double wedding."

Millie looked up at Dorothy. Dorothy nodded her head and blushed. "He asked me last night too," she murmured.

"Double wedding, good organization," Trevor Graydon said. "The moon and the stars . . ." his voice trailed off.

"Now that that's settled, kids, I'll be off for my lesson." Muzzy stood up in her trim blue uniform. She kissed them all good-bye and walked out humming a little marching song. Through the French doors they watched her greet the handsome police sergeant with a firm handclasp.

"Like a squirrel storing the nuts of life," Millie said. "What a wonderful step-grandmother she'll make." Then Millie blushed prettily at her own daring but deliciously old-fashioned thought.

THE END

## ABOUT THE AUTHOR

HILA COLMAN has written more than a dozen novels for girls, as well as innumerable magazine articles and stories which have appeared in *Seventeen*, *Ingenue*, *McCall's* and *Redbook*.

**Your Key to the Year's Most Exciting Reading Experience**